WISHFUL TAILS

THE WISHING TREE SERIES BOOK 15

BARBARA HINSKE

PRAISE FOR BARBARA HINSKE

Know an author who can grab you on the very first page so that you HAVE to keep reading? If not, then you must read Barbara Hinske. –Amazon Reviewer

Barbara Hinske writes the most engaging stories that you just cannot put down. –Amazon Reviewer

Barbara Hinske always introduces characters that become your friends and sets her novels so that you are immediately drawn in and your interest is held to the end, which is always neatly tied together, often in a surprising and unexpected way. –Amazon Reviewer

Barbara Hinske has written another warm and gentle book about people who care. The story reminds the reader

Wishful Tails
by Barbara Hinske

ISBN: 9798987694282

LCCN: 2024907960

Casa del Northern Publishing

Phoenix, Arizona

For our wonderful readers in My Book Friends.

ALSO BY BARBARA HINSKE

Available at Amazon in Print, Audio, and for Kindle

The Rosemont Series

Coming to Rosemont

Weaving the Strands

Uncovering Secrets

Drawing Close

Bringing Them Home

Shelving Doubts

Restoring What Was Lost

No Matter How Far

When Dreams There Be

Novellas

The Night Train

The Christmas Club (adapted
for The Hallmark Channel, 2019)

Paws & Pastries

Sweets & Treats

Snowflakes, Cupcakes & Kittens

Workout Wishes & Valentine Kisses

Wishes of Home

Wishful Tails

Novels in the Guiding Emily Series

Guiding Emily (adapted for The Hallmark Channel, 2023)

The Unexpected Path

Over Every Hurdle

Down the Aisle

From the Heart

Novels in the "Who's There?!" Collection

Deadly Parcel

Final Circuit

CHAPTER 1

a sudden gust of wind caught the balloon arch and sent it scraping against the Duncan's Hardware sign. One pop and then another signaled the demise of two more balloons. Jed Duncan peered out the double glass door that served as the entrance to Linden Falls' venerable hardware store. "Look at that sky," he said, pointing to the rapidly gathering mass of dark clouds. "We'll be lucky to have any balloons left by the time we make the announcement."

"This storm wasn't supposed to arrive until late tonight," replied Marty Beckman. The director of *Wishes of Home,* the popular home-improvement television show sponsored by Duncan's Hardware, checked his watch. "We're scheduled to film in fifteen minutes. I think the arch will hold together until then. And if our co-hosts arrive early, my crew is ready. We can roll as soon as they're here."

Another burst of wind took out another three balloons.

"I want to wait until the newspaper is here to cover the reveal of the second season of the show. Laura Thompson, the little girl whose idea was chosen for the project, should arrive right after school gets out. That's why we chose 3:30. It wouldn't be right to start without Laura."

Marty eyed the massing clouds. "If it starts raining, we can move the announcement inside." He looked around himself, searching for an appropriate spot. "It's packed in here. I'm not sure where we'd move to. Maybe your office?"

Jed shook his head. "Too ordinary. I want the shot at the entrance, with the Duncan's Hardware name prominently displayed." He continued to squint at the town square across the street from his store.

A couple, bent at the waist with arms close to their sides, entered the square at the far end and marched resolutely into the wind.

"That's them," Jed said, tapping the glass of the door. "Pam and Steve are coming across the square now."

"Excellent." Marty checked his watch. "It's 3:20.

We'll do our final light and sound checks with them and be ready to go as soon as Laura gets here."

A smattering of raindrops hit the glass and zigzagged down the length of the door.

Pam Olson and Steve Turner reached the curb on the other side of the street and stopped to allow a car to pass by. Pam pulled the hood of her jacket over her hair and held it in place under her chin. As soon as the car was gone, they sprinted across the street.

Jed flung the door open for them as the drizzle turned into a steady stream.

Pam rushed inside, followed closely by Steve. The wind slammed the door shut with a resounding thwack.

Pam pushed her hood away from her face. "Wow. It wasn't even cloudy when we decided to walk over from the gym. I can't believe this."

Jed groaned and put his hand to his head.

Pam looked at Jed and patted her friend's back reassuringly. "Don't worry. We'll film in the rain if need be. We can hold umbrellas—like we did in that one episode last season. It's all going to be fine."

"Do you still have umbrellas with the Duncan's Hardware logo?" Steve asked.

"I always stock them. I'll go get a couple." Jed walked toward an end cap at the back of the store.

"I hate seeing Jed so deflated," Pam said to Marty and Steve. "He's been beyond excited to reveal this project."

Additional popping outside the door signaled the demise of still more balloons.

"We could always delay the announcement for a couple of weeks. I know Jed wants to start filming the season soon, but that can't happen until the land is acquired, architectural plans are completed, and building permits are obtained. That'll be weeks— maybe months," Steve said.

Marty shook his head. "That's what I told him earlier when the storm began moving in early. He insists the announcement has to be today."

Pam shrugged. "Jed has to have a reason. We'll make it work."

"If that balloon arch gets torn off the building, it'll add drama to the shot," Steve quipped.

Jed rejoined them, carrying an armload of umbrellas.

An SUV parked at the curb two doors down from Duncan's Hardware. Ten-year-old Laura Thompson and her mother got out of the car and raced to the store. The rain stopped and a ray of sunshine slashed through the clouds as they pulled open the door at 3:29.

The little girl entered and stepped into Pam's

waiting arms. "Look at you!" Pam cried, giving her a hug. "You bring sunshine with you wherever you go."

Laura's mother laughed. "She insisted—during the entire drive over here from school—that everything would be okay. And it is." She untied the pink ribbon that was Laura's signature hair ornament and corralled the curly blonde wisps that the wind had dislodged before retying a neat bow.

"I'm so glad I can finally talk about this," Laura said.

"Me too," Pam said. "It was hard knowing—and having to keep—the secret."

"I'm really proud of Laura," her mom said. "I almost spilled the beans yesterday."

"This break in the weather may not last." Marty interrupted and motioned for everyone to assemble under the balloon arch. "You ready?" he asked his crew, who huddled in the narrow alcove around the door.

The newspaper reporter stood with the crew, his pencil and notebook at the ready.

The cameraman, soundman, and the rest of the crew were in position before Jed joined the others under the arch.

He clutched a sheet of lined yellow paper, torn from a legal pad.

"Do you need to hold that, Jed?" Marty asked. "It'll look better if you don't need notes."

Jed swallowed hard.

"Speak from your heart," Pam said. "I know you. It's all in there." She tapped her own heart.

"She's right, my friend," Marty said. "You've got this." He held out his hand for the yellow paper.

Jed ran his eyes along the page, then surrendered it to the director.

Marty smiled at him reassuringly, then positioned Jed on one end, Steve on the other, and Pam and Laura between them.

Thunder rumbled in the distance.

"Let's see if we can do this in one take," Marty called from the edge of the sidewalk. "Smile, everybody."

A crew member snapped the film clapper.

Jed took a deep breath and began.

"Today is a very special day for Linden Falls. The dream of this young lady ..." he leaned over and smiled into Laura's upturned face, "is going to come true. And this dream will save lives and enrich our community."

Jed straightened and spoke into the camera. "Laura Thompson entered the contest here at Duncan's Hardware to suggest the project for the second season of *Wishes of Home*. She not only entered our contest, but she also tied a wish onto our very own Wishing Tree. Anyone who's lived in Linden Falls for long knows the power of wishes tied to that tree."

He paused for a beat, and his voice resonated with enthusiasm when he spoke again. "*Wishes of Home* will build a no-kill animal shelter right here in Linden Falls!"

Laura bounced on her heels. Her grin stretched out of sight on either side of her face.

"We've selected the location and have obtained permits to begin construction right away."

Pam and Steve's heads jerked up in unison. They both looked at Jed with wide eyes.

"This last news is a surprise for our hosts, Pam Olson and Steve Turner. And for our director." Jed chuckled. "Duncan's Hardware owns a large warehouse building on the outskirts of town. It's situated on ten wooded acres. We haven't used it since we moved into our new warehouse behind the store. We considered selling it, but my grandfather started this business from that location, and I'm sentimental. I couldn't let it go. When the idea of building a no-kill animal shelter came up, I knew it would be the perfect spot."

Pam slipped her arm around his back and gave Jed a side hug.

"My grandfather never met a dog or cat he didn't like. I know he'd be thrilled about this new life for the property. There's still plenty of work to be done to make it into a shelter. The outside shell of the 60,000 square foot building is solid, but a lot of interior improvements need to be done."

Jed took a step forward. "Here's where you come in. Duncan's will supply all the materials, but we'd like community volunteers—working on the weekends—to do the construction work. We'll film on the weekends. We also need input on what services we should provide, and other uses for the property. I'm not an expert on any of this. I've looked online, and there are all kinds of fun things we could use the property for—all centering on our beloved four-legged friends." A smile came to his face, as if channeling the pleasure he knew his grandfather would feel.

"If you're interested in lending a hand with construction or would like to suggest uses for the property, please let me know."

Laura's tiny hand shot straight into the air, her hand twisting like a pinwheel in the wind.

Jed laughed. "I think we have our first volunteer. Do you want to help come up with ideas or help build?" he asked the little girl.

"Both," she cried.

Everyone laughed.

"If you're interested, there are sign-up sheets in the store, at the registers. Thank you for making *Wishes of Home* such a success. I can't wait to work with everyone in this community to make our new shelter a reality."

Jed took a step back.

Marty motioned to the cameraman to pull back and widen the shot. A rainbow sliced across the sky above Duncan's Hardware.

CHAPTER 2

*P*am stuck her head into the trainers' break room at Linden Falls Fitness. She knew Steve had a break between clients and expected to find him nestled into the broken-down sofa with a steaming cup of black coffee.

Steve sat on the sofa, hunched forward over his phone, with his thumbs flying over the keypad on the screen.

"Did you see?" Pam asked.

Steve's head jerked up. He stopped typing and pulled his phone into his chest. "Sorry—did I see what?"

"Marty texted the filming schedule. He wants to film meetings with the volunteers and community members who have ideas about additional ways to use the property. We're supposed to moderate the discussions."

"Okay," Steve responded, glancing at the screen of his phone before swiping away from whatever he'd been looking at.

"I'm no good at that," Pam said. She sighed in exasperation at his blank expression. "Moderating meetings?"

"I'm sure you'd be great at it, but I can take the lead."

"Good. That's what I wanted to hear. I've been at library board meetings, and people in Linden Falls can be very opinionated."

"I think that's known as Yankee stubbornness."

"Whatever. I don't want to manage it."

"You won't have to." Steve scooched over and patted the sofa next to him.

"I can't. I've got another client in …" Pam looked at her watch, "three minutes."

"When does all this filming start?"

"A week from Saturday," Pam said. "Thanks for putting my mind at ease. I've gotta go." She stepped away without noticing his crestfallen expression.

He raked his fingers through his hair. There was nothing for it—he'd have to cancel the romantic dinner for two he'd just booked at the end of the month. He'd been on the waiting list for a reservation at the Michelin-starred restaurant for over a month and had been thrilled when he'd gotten the text about an opening.

Steve knew from experience that, once filming began, they'd both be too tired from their day jobs as personal trainers and their side hustle as hosts of *Wishes of Home* to even be remotely interested in going out of town for a fancy dinner. He'd have to think of something else—and he'd need to do it this Sunday. He typed the cancellation and tapped send.

Handling the other big issue wouldn't be easy. He'd approved the design her mother had assured him Pam would love, but that was only ten days ago. They'd promised him it would be ready in three weeks. Could he persuade them to make it this Sunday?

Steve scrolled through his contacts and placed his call. The owner had been a client for years. He prayed his warm, personal relationship would persuade the woman to move his order to the top of the list.

CHAPTER 3

"I'm glad we got here extra early to set up," Pam said, glancing over her shoulder at the people streaming onto the Linden Falls town square. "We're going to be swamped."

"The first farmers market of the season is always busy. People are tired of being cooped up inside all winter." Irene Olson took a step back to admire the racks of brightly colored aprons and tables stacked with her handmade placemats, table runners, napkins, and tablecloths. "The booth looks good, doesn't it?"

"Fabulous! You've outdone yourself, Mom. I'm glad you used your downtime this winter to sew plenty of inventory. This stuff will sell like hotcakes."

Irene slipped her arm around her daughter's waist. "I hope you're right."

"I love that new line of dog collars and bandanas." Pam pointed to a display stand at the back of the stall. "They're adorable! I already set aside the one with rabbits chasing each other down the center for Chance. I'll pay for it before I leave."

"You'll do no such thing. That'll be my thank you for coming out early to help me today."

"I love working the market with you," Pam said. "Always have. I just wish you'd listen to my suggestion to move the dog items up front. They'll draw people into your booth."

"We'll see," Irene replied. "If they sell, we can move the display. I've tried to expand my inventory beyond table linens before and it hasn't gone well."

"These will sell. I'll bet we move them within the hour," Pam said.

Irene looked at her watch. "We open in one minute."

"Thank goodness last week's storm was followed by a perfect spring weekend." Pam took her usual spot in the back of the booth while her mother stepped behind a table in the front.

"Good morning," Irene said to a young woman holding the hand of a toddler. "Can I help you find anything?"

"I'm looking for a table runner and placemats for my Easter table. I'm hosting brunch this year."

"You can go with holiday-themed linens or generic ones in spring colors and patterns."

"I'd like to see both."

Irene drew her to a table on the far side of the booth. "I'll leave you to browse," she said. "Let me know if you need any help."

The woman nodded absently, her attention absorbed by the colorful offerings.

Pam and Irene worked at a fever pitch until a lull in mid-morning. "Whew! I don't ever remember being this busy." Irene brushed her hair away from her face and tucked it behind her ears. "Even the weekend before Christmas isn't this bad."

"I was thinking the same thing." Pam pointed to the display of dog items where a solitary collar dangled from a hook. "Unless you've got more in the car, there's no point in moving the display to the front."

Irene shifted her gaze to Pam. "You're right. They sold like hotcakes. I hadn't noticed." She clasped her hands together. "I'm glad. I use fabric scraps to make them, and they go together fast, so they cost me next to nothing to produce. My plan is to donate my profits from the sales of the dog stuff to the new shelter."

"That's very generous of you, Mom."

"I've got more in a plastic tote in the back of my

car," Irene said. "Would you mind retrieving them before we get busy again?"

"Not at all. I'd like to go to the ladies' room, too. I'll help you restock table linens from the totes underneath the tables and then I'll fetch the pup paraphernalia."

"I can refill the tables. You scoot to the ladies' and then bring back more dog inventory."

"I'll hurry," Pam said. "It looks like another wave of people is arriving." She jogged toward the restroom building at the corner of the square.

Irene restocked her tables with the speed and precision of someone who had been doing it for decades. When she was satisfied, she shielded her eyes with her hand and scanned the crowd, searching for her daughter. Pam was walking toward her at a fast clip, clutching a large plastic tote to her chest.

As her eyes continued to search the crowd, Irene noticed the familiar figure of a tall, dark-haired young man exiting Linden Falls' venerable jeweler. She smiled to herself. She hoped he'd picked up the item she'd collaborated with him on—and that she would have something wonderful to celebrate with her daughter. Soon.

Pam arrived at the booth as Irene was ringing up another large order. She placed the tote on the ground and moved the now empty display stand to a prominent spot in front. Unpacking the tote and placing collars and bandanas on the display proved to be like plugging the proverbial hole in the dam: customers removed them as soon as she hung them up—and some even took them out of her hands.

By the time the market closed at two o'clock, every dog item had been sold, along with eighty percent of the other inventory.

Pam and Irene replaced the unsold items in their totes and hauled them, the display tables and stands, and the tent to Irene's car with the efficiency of a circus packing up to leave town.

Irene shut the hatchback and leaned against the side of the car. "I can't believe that. What a morning!"

"I'll bet this will be your biggest day ever."

"I think so. I'm eager to tally it up."

"You sold out of the dog items."

"I know." Irene hugged herself. "I'm thrilled. That means I made $1,000 for the new shelter."

"Maybe the shelter should have a gift shop. You could sell them there, too."

"That's a great idea."

"There's a meeting in a couple of weeks to solicit community input on other uses for the property. Steve and I will be there, but I don't want to make suggestions. Will you come to suggest a gift shop?"

"I heard about the meeting and planned to attend —out of curiosity. If you really think it's a good idea, I'll suggest it."

"I do."

"Then I'll bring it up at the meeting." She regarded her daughter. "Are you and Steve going out tonight?"

"No. He's got meetings about the soccer league all afternoon and is coordinating with his replacement afterward."

Irene arched an eyebrow.

"With the upcoming filming of season two on the weekends, he can't run the spring soccer league. A parent who's had older kids go through the program is taking over for Steve—at least for this year."

"I'm glad to hear it. You're both far too busy. Between your personal training clients and hosting *Wishes of Home*, you each have two full-time jobs."

"It sometimes feels that way."

"Are you seeing each other this weekend?"

"We're going into the country for a picnic tomorrow. He's picking me up at nine and we're spending the day."

"That sounds wonderful. It's supposed to be another nice day tomorrow."

"I'm looking forward to it. It'll be lovely to be out in nature. We're taking Chance with us. Steve says he knows the perfect place."

"Are you packing the picnic?"

Pam shook her head. "Steve said he's got it all handled. He doesn't want me to fuss. I'm to get a good night's sleep and to wear hiking boots."

"Ah …"

"He's been very secretive about his plan," Pam said. "I can tell he's very excited, too. I think it's incredibly sweet."

Irene suppressed a grin. She hoped she knew why Steve was excited.

"What're you doing this afternoon?" Pam asked.

"I've got a quick errand to run and then I'm going home to sew more collars."

"Can I join you? I'd like to help."

"I'd love that. There's a crock-pot of homemade chicken noodle soup on the counter. I baked sugar cookies yesterday using those new gnome cookie cutters I told you about, and I plan to decorate them after supper. I'm taking them to book club tomorrow afternoon."

"How fun!"

"Will you stay for supper? If you help me decorate cookies, you can take some on your picnic."

"That's a terrific plan. I don't like the idea of

being empty-handed when Steve shows up tomorrow."

"Then it's settled."

"I'll swing by my house to feed Leopold and then I'll come over."

"I'll be home by then. My errand won't take long," Irene said.

"I'm off. See you soon." Pam headed to her car.

Irene watched her walk, then pulled a piece of paper and pen out of her purse. She wrote her wish on the paper, found a piece of ribbon from the extra sewing supplies she kept in her car, and headed back to the town square.

The Wishing Tree needed a new wish. One that would change the life of her beloved daughter.

CHAPTER 4

Steve snapped the lid shut and hid the small, blue velvet box in a kitchen cupboard behind boxes of Bisquick and baking soda that had expired years earlier. He inhaled slowly. He thought it was gorgeous, but would she?

"What do you think, boy?" Steve reached down to stroke the enormous black Lab who had been his shadow since the moment Pam had given the dog to him. Chance rested his muzzle against Steve's thigh and rolled his brown eyes to meet his master's gaze.

"She surprised me with you, and it turns out that you're the best gift I've ever had. I hope she loves the ring as much as I do you."

He continued petting his dog. "Or should I have listened to my sister? Carol told me to let Pam pick out her own ring."

Chance's gaze remained locked on Steve.

"But Pam's a traditionalist," Steve continued. "I want to have a ring to present. We're going on a picnic tomorrow and I'm going to pop the question there. If she doesn't like it, the jeweler promised me we could exchange it."

Chance raised a paw and tapped Steve's leg.

"Since it's going to be such a nice day, you can come with us. Heck—she loves you so much, it'll increase my chances of her saying yes if you're there."

Chance uttered a short "Woof."

Steve laughed. "You don't have to agree with that, buddy." He grabbed his keys from the kitchen counter and headed toward the door to his garage. "Let's drive into the country. I have an hour and a half until I have to be at the soccer meeting. I want to scope out a couple of places for our picnic."

Chance trotted after his master.

"We're on a mission, boy. Let's look for trees, wildflowers, a stone wall—bonus points for a bubbling brook; any old place won't do."

Chance emitted a more definite bark.

"I knew you'd understand," Steve said, clipping a leash on Chance's collar. "Let's find a spot we'll remember for the rest of our lives."

～

"My gosh, Mom," Pam said, pointing to the stack of dog collars she'd just stowed in a plastic tote. "We made three dozen collars in a little under two hours."

"It really helped that you cut all the fabric and assembled them with the backing material and the metal hardware. All I had to do was run them through the sewing machine." Irene reached over and patted her daughter's hand. "Working together was more than twice as fast as making them alone."

"I may not have time to help when we're filming again. Do you want to keep going now?"

Irene shook her head. "My eyes are shot for tonight and I'm hungry. I think it's time to call it quits and eat."

"That soup smells amazing," Pam said.

"Will you dish each of us a bowl—and I'll toast slices of that loaf of sourdough bread I bought at the market?"

"With pleasure."

The two women moved to Irene's cozy kitchen and got busy. A carefully curated selection of small appliances crowded the limited countertops. An old bean crock stood next to the stove, corralling a well-worn selection of wooden spoons, spatulas, whisks, and tongs arranged like flowers in a vase.

"Are we eating in here?" Pam gestured toward the small kitchen table dressed in a tablecloth featuring branches of dogwood blossoms.

Irene nodded.

"This is still my favorite tablecloth of all time," Pam said.

"It's practically threadbare," Irene said. "I should replace it, but I can't bear to. Your grandmother made it for me as a wedding shower gift. I guess I'm a sentimental fool."

"That's where I get it from, then," Pam said, setting the bowls of soup on the table, their aromatic steam filling the room. "Tea?" The question was probably unnecessary. She and her mother always drank tea when they were together.

The toast popped up and Irene buttered it while Pam set the kettle to boil.

Irene took a plate of toast to the table and sank into a chair. "Would you take the icing out of the fridge to soften a bit before we decorate the cookies? It's in the icing bags, ready to go."

Pam did as her mother asked. "We've got white and three shades of green." She looked at her mother. "Are we making St. Patrick's Day troll cookies?"

"That's the plan. If that doesn't appeal to you, we can make more icing after dinner, and you can color it any way you want."

"Are you kidding? I love the idea of adorable, green troll cookies. This is going to be so much fun."

"I thought the book club gals would get a kick out of them."

Pam brought two cups of tea to the table, and they fell silent as they enjoyed the simple but delicious meal.

"Soup for supper is so good," Pam said, sighing with contentment as she rose to fill her bowl again. "Do you want more?"

"Why not? Just one ladleful."

When they'd stuffed themselves with soup and bread, they cleared the table and loaded the dishwasher. Irene brought the rectangular container holding the cookies to the table.

"Do you have pictures to follow or are we doing this free-form?" Pam asked.

"Gracious," Irene said. "I was going to pipe on a hat and a beard, add dots of other shades of green, and call it a day."

Pam was already scrolling through photos on her phone. "I think we can do better than that." She held out the screen to her mother. "Do you like these guys?"

"They're little works of art. Do you think we can make ours look like those?"

"Yeah. The website says all you need is a small, round tip. Nothing fancy. These are disposable icing bags, so we'll snip a tiny bit off the end to make our tip. I think this will be easy."

"I'm game to try if you are. I have plenty of ingredients to make more icing. If we don't like what we've created, we can scrape it off and start over."

"That's the spirit, Mom." Pam selected a cookie that looked like a troll with an elongated, skinny hat. She picked up the bag of light green icing, carefully cut off the end, outlined the hat, and then filled it in with icing.

"That looks good," Irene said. "How did you know to do that?"

"I watch episodes of *The Great British Baking Show* over and over. I guess I've learned a few things." She moved on to create a plaited beard with white icing.

"I'm going to do what you do," Irene said and copied her daughter.

"We need a bag with light pink icing—for noses. Gnomes have big noses," Pam said.

"You're absolutely right. I've got extra white icing. I'll tint it and make a bag." Irene was soon back with the necessary ingredient.

The duo worked in companionable silence, adding shamrocks, stars, polka dots, and bow ties to the growing army of trolls—all with bulbous pink noses. When they placed the final cookie on the drying rack, they leaned back to admire their work.

Pam held the screen of her phone next to their cookies. "We did a fantastic job of copying these, don't you think?"

"Absolutely. They're charming. Book club is going to be impressed."

She swiveled her face to look at her mother. "Did you enjoy doing this?"

"Absolutely. Take a picture of them."

Pam snapped a handful of photos from a distance and close up. "I have a new appreciation of why decorated cookies in a bakery are so expensive. These are a labor of love."

"That's a good point," Irene said. "Decorating three dozen was fun; ten or twelve dozen would be a different story."

"Should we each eat one?" Pam asked. "Quality control and all that?"

"It's the responsible thing to do." Irene gave her daughter a conspiratorial smile. "We don't want to give them to others if they're horrible."

"Let's eat our worst one."

They each selected a cookie and took a bite.

Pam moaned. "It's so buttery and creamy. Even Paul Hollywood would say it's a perfect bake."

Irene chuckled. "The ratio of icing to cookie is just right, too."

The grandfather clock in the entryway chimed ten.

"Good grief—look at the time," Irene said. She jumped out of her chair and grabbed the rectangular, plastic storage box. "Let's get your cookies boxed up so you can get home."

"It's not that late, Mom. I'm never in bed before eleven."

"Maybe that's why you're always so tired," Irene chided. "I'm asleep by this time."

Irene began carefully placing Pam's cookies into the container.

"Isn't this the box for the cookies you're taking to book club?"

"I have another one just like it," Irene said.

"I don't need a dozen and a half," Pam said.

"With that man of yours around? I think Steve could eat a dozen at one sitting."

Pam laughed. "You're right about that."

Irene stole a glance at her daughter. "Take them with you on your picnic tomorrow. They'll bring you luck."

Pam stifled a yawn and stood. "I guess I *am* tired." She took the box of cookies her mother handed her. "Thank you for dinner—and for these."

Irene pulled Pam into a hug and held her tight. "Enjoy everything about your day tomorrow."

CHAPTER 5

Steve went over Chance's coat with a brush one last time before snapping the leash on his collar. He checked his own reflection in the mirror, smoothed his hair into place, and patted his jacket pocket for the thousandth time to be certain the ring box was in his inner pocket.

"Okay, boy. Let's *do* this thing."

They headed to his SUV and made the short drive to Pam's house. His dashboard clock showed they were ten minutes early. Pam was never ready early. He should wait in the driveway instead of racing to the door, but he was too excited to cool his heels for even five minutes.

Steve got out of his SUV and headed for her door, leaving Chance behind to smudge his rear windows with nose prints. He had his foot on the first step when Pam threw the door open.

"You're early. I'm almost ready." Pam pulled a wide-toothed comb through her chestnut curls. "I saw you pull in from my bedroom window. Can you bring Chance in for a minute? I have a surprise for him."

The sight of her left him, as it always did, dumb-struck. Even with no makeup and her hair pulled back in a ponytail, Pam was the most beautiful woman he'd ever seen. Now—with her hair curling around her shoulders and a light dusting of makeup to accentuate her features—she was dazzling.

Pam stopped her comb mid-stroke. "Is that okay? If Chance comes in?"

"Oh … sure."

Pam disappeared into the house, leaving the door open.

Steve reversed course and was soon standing in the foyer with Chance at his side.

Leopold, Pam's cat, hopped onto the entryway table and glared at Chance.

The friendly dog approached him, extending his nose to sniff the agile, furry creature.

As Pam came around the corner with a shopping bag in hand, the cat hissed and swatted Chance's nose with claws extended.

Chance yelped, more in protest than in pain.

"Leopold!" Pam snatched her cat from the table. "That's not nice! Chance is our friend. We don't treat friends that way."

Leopold slanted his eyes to his owner and glared through slits.

"I mean it. You're going to the laundry room until you can be friendly to Chance." She stalked off down the hall, opened a door, and unceremoniously deposited the cat inside before closing the door.

"I'm so sorry!" she said, rushing back to the foyer where Steve was examining Chance's nose. "Did he do any damage?"

"No." Steve ruffled Chance's ears. "I think his feelings are more hurt than anything else. He doesn't understand why anyone doesn't like him."

Pam dropped to her knees and threw her arms around the big Lab. "You're such a good boy and Leopold is a big baby. He'll come around and love you, just like I do. It's just going to take time."

She stood and removed the collar she'd bought for him at the market and held it out to the dog. "My mom made this," she said. "See all the friendly bunnies chasing each other?" She ran her finger along the collar as she showed it to Chance. "You'll look great in this. Do you like it?"

Steve chuckled. "I'm sure he does."

"Can we put it on him? I can get pliers so you can remove his tags from the collar he's wearing and put them on this one."

"I won't need pliers." Steve unbuckled Chance's collar and pulled the rings apart to insert the tags on the new collar. "Do you want to do the honors?" he said, holding the new collar out to Pam.

She adjusted the size and buckled it in place. "There. Aren't you handsome?"

"I'll take a picture of the two of you to send your mom."

"She'll love that. Make sure the collar shows." Pam knelt close to Chance. "He smells wonderful. Did you just give him a bath?"

"I sure did. We both got spiffed up for our day."

Pam stood and wrapped her arms around Steve, nuzzling his neck. "Is that aftershave I smell?"

"It is." Steve brushed kisses along her temple.

"I've never known you to wear it." She breathed in. "It's nice."

"As I said, we both got cleaned up for today."

They shared an unhurried kiss.

Pam stepped back out of his arms. "I'm casual—like you said. Sneakers and jeans. Should I change into something nicer?"

"You're perfect. And I love your hair down."

"I decided I needed something different than my weekday ponytail."

"I love your ponytail, don't get me wrong," Steve paused, aware that he might be on shaky ground, expressing an opinion on her hair, "but your hair is so beautiful. I love seeing it loose."

Pam punched his shoulder lightly. "Good answer. Now—let's get out of here. This may be the last leisurely Sunday we have in a very long time." She picked up the rectangular container of cookies and pulled her purse off the hook by the door.

"What's in there?" Steve asked.

"A little surprise Mom and I made last night."

"Can I see?"

"You'll have to wait until the picnic." Her cool smile belied the excitement she felt about showing him her creations.

Steve grasped Chance's leash and opened the door. He struggled to keep his face devoid of emotion. Pam wasn't the only one with a secret to reveal.

PAM STOOD in the dappled sunshine of a line of trees bordering a grassy field dotted with yellow and white wildflowers. She shielded her eyes with her hand as she turned her face in an arch, examining the tranquil setting in front of her.

"I can't believe how beautiful this is." She closed her eyes and inhaled deeply through her nose. "The air even smells cleaner. And listen." She stopped talking and remained silent. "The only sounds are birds chirping, insects buzzing, and the wind rustling through the trees. We're truly alone with all this."

Steve came up behind her and circled her with his arms, resting his chin on the top of her head. "It's exactly as I remember it."

Pam leaned back against him. "You've been here before?"

"Yes—as a kid."

"Can we set up over there?" Pam pointed to a level patch of ground shaded by a tree at the edge of a swath of wildflowers.

"I don't see any 'No Trespassing' signs." Steve bent to pick up the hamper of delicacies he'd purchased at the upscale grocery in the next town and the blanket he'd brought for them.

Pam grasped her container of cookies and Chance's leash.

They set off to the spot that would hold a very special place in their hearts.

CHAPTER 6

*L*aura set the last coffee can aside and admired her handiwork. Her mom had cut a slot in each of the plastic lids large enough to accommodate folded money. Then Laura had spray-painted each can white and had carefully applied felt stickers that looked like paw prints. An oval picture frame had been attached to each can. Right now, they each held a photo of an adorable dog or cat.

"Those look very professional," her mother said. "I love the photos of the pets. Extremely eye catching."

"Thanks, Mom. When the shelter opens, we can change the photo out for one of the animals we have up for adoption."

"That's a great idea, honey! We'll take photos with my phone and print them out here."

"When the animal is adopted, I'll change the photo to another one looking for a home. I'll have to keep lists for that." Laura opened a spiral-bound notebook with the word SHELTER scrawled across the front, each letter in a different color, and made a note.

Her mother smiled at the little girl with the giant brain and even bigger heart. "You amaze me with your organizational skills, sweetheart. And your creativity and determination. One day, you'll be the CEO of a big organization."

"I want to be a veterinarian," Laura said, flipping a page in her notebook. "Or a Lego master."

Her mother chuckled. "You'd be great at either one. You may come up with something completely different, too." Her mother came up behind her and leaned over her shoulder. "Is that the list of businesses that have agreed to put your donation cans for the no-kill shelter at their registers?"

Laura nodded. "We've got Duncan's Hardware, The Wishing Tree Inn, Woody's Pizza, the Crooked Porch Cafe, and Town Square Books."

"That's a great start. I'm sure Millie King at the office supply store will let you put one in her shop.

She's an animal lover—I see her and her golden retriever all over town."

"Can we go see her after school this week?"

"Sure."

"I'll bet Pam will get approval to put one at Linden Falls Fitness, too," Laura said.

"Good idea. That place is always busy. We'll have to pick up donations regularly," her mother said. "Is that on one of your lists?"

Laura turned a page in her notebook. "That's when I can change pet photos on the collection can."

"I think you've thought of everything. It's a beautiful Sunday afternoon. Let's deliver these cans, then stop off for an ice cream."

Laura hopped out of her chair. "I hope we see Gladys in town today. She's my favorite dog—aside from Rusty."

Laura's mother began placing the decorated coffee cans in a cardboard box they'd gotten on their last visit to the gigantic membership store on the outskirts of town. "She's awfully sweet. If we got another dog, would you want a golden retriever?"

"*Can* we get another dog?" Laura vibrated with excitement. "It'll be from the new shelter, and it'll be one we're meant to have. But you and Dad always said no to another dog."

"We've been talking about it since you've been so

committed to this shelter project. You're extremely responsible with Rusty, and we never have to remind you to feed him or walk him." Her mother drew her in for a hug. "A future veterinarian should grow up with dogs."

"I was going to ask the Wishing Tree for another one." Laura pulled a scrap of paper from underneath her notebook. "I've got my wish all ready to hang on the tree."

Her mother patted Laura on the back and swallowed hard. "We can do that today. Just remember, sometimes it takes a while for those wishes to come true."

"It won't," Laura said. "I can feel it. We'll find our dog at the shelter."

CHAPTER 7

a tree stood at the edge of the field like a jewel in a crown, its newly-sprouted leaves a vibrant green against the lapis sky. Steve spread a plaid camping blanket in its shade.

Pam deposited the container of cookies on one corner. "I've always wanted to do this," she said before dropping Chance's leash and racing into the field. She flung her arms open at shoulder height and walked in a slow circle through the tall grass.

Steve placed the hamper next to the cookies and stood to watch.

Tilting her head back, she opened her mouth and sang. "The hills are alive ..."

Chance bounded up to her as she continued the song. He jumped up on her, but she ignored him, engrossed in her task as she mimicked Julie Andrews in the famous opening scene from *The Sound of Music*. He got a case of the zoomies and zigzagged across the field.

Pam pretended she heard a church bell, placed her hand on the top of her head, and raced to Steve.

He stopped clapping and opened his arms to her. "That was great! I didn't know you could sing."

Pam nestled against him. "It never came up."

He leaned back to look at her. "I'm serious—that was fantastic."

"I was a theater kid," she shrugged. "I was cast as Liesl my sophomore year of college and was the understudy for Maria. Our Maria never missed a show and I never got to perform the role. That was so disappointing. I don't know what came over me just now. I couldn't stop myself." She smiled into his eyes. "Do you think I'm a complete kook?"

He cupped her chin with his hand. "I think you're the most authentic, fun, creative person I've ever met. I'm thrilled you're comfortable enough with me to be yourself."

Pam chuckled. "You may regret saying that. There are several more songs from that show I'm dying to sing."

"Then I hope you do. I'd love that."

"My singing got Chance all fired up." Pam

shielded her eyes from the sun and searched for Chance. "Speaking of which, where'd he go?"

"He's probably chasing a rabbit or squirrel." Steve put two fingers in his mouth and gave a sharp whistle.

A furry black speck bounded out of the trees at the edge of the field, then disappeared again.

"He's fine," Steve said. "Are you hungry? We can unpack the hamper."

Pam bit her lip. "It makes me nervous that we can't see Chance. Let's go get him and bring him back with us."

Steve cupped his hands around his mouth and hollered for Chance.

The dog did not reappear.

Pam began walking toward the spot where they'd last seen him. Steve joined her, periodically calling his dog—without response.

They finally reached the edge of the field where they'd last seen the dog. A chain-link fence separated the field from the trees on the other side.

Steve whistled for the dog, and this time Chance bounded up to them—on the other side of the fence.

"How in the heck did you get over there, boy?" Steve asked rhetorically.

Chance wagged his tail.

"He couldn't have jumped this fence," Pam said.

"No. There must be an opening somewhere along here."

"You silly boy," Pam said, reaching her fingers through the links to scratch the nose he extended to her.

"It can't be far," Steve said.

They began walking along the fence, with Chance mirroring their progress on the other side. They'd gone no more than ten yards when Pam found the gap between two sections of fencing.

Chance watched them, his front legs extended into a downward dog pose, his tail wagging mightily.

"I think he's inviting us inside," Pam said.

Before Steve could respond, Pam squeezed herself through the opening. She turned back to Steve, with Chance at her side.

"Now you're both on the wrong side," Steve said.

"Join us," Pam said.

Steve tried to pass through the opening and failed. "The two of you had better come back to me."

"I can see the top of a chimney," Pam said, pointing behind her.

"There's a big ole house back there. My best friend's great-grandfather owned it and the surrounding acreage. We used to play here as kids. I always loved that place."

"Does the family still live there?"

Steve shook his head. "They kept it after the old man died, as a summer place. It had been a dairy farm. They sold the herd and eventually the property. I drove by yesterday afternoon to see if I could find it and if we could have our picnic here. The house has become some sort of venue. They call it Enchanted Grove Estate."

"That's a pretty name. Sounds like a wedding venue."

Steve's breath caught in his throat. "You're probably right."

"Is the meadow where we spread out our picnic still part of the venue's property?"

"I have no idea."

Pam reached her hand through the opening in the fence and grasped his, drawing him toward her. "Climb the fence and the three of us will go check it out," she coaxed.

"I believe we're trespassing."

"I call it exploring. If it's a venue, we're not invading someone's back yard. We won't do any damage, and no one is going to arrest us."

Steve looked into the pleading eyes of the woman he loved, and hoisted himself up and over the fence. "This is another side of you I'm seeing. You're very nosey, aren't you?"

"I prefer to call myself curious. Just like Chance, here. Huh, boy?" She ruffled his ears.

"Just a quick look, okay? Then we'll turn around and get out."

"Absolutely."

"It's coming back to me now. This way." He pointed to his right and headed through a stand of trees with Pam and Chance at his heels.

The rear elevation of a two-story house came into view like pieces being placed in a puzzle. A massive stone fireplace dominated one side of the home. Windows with pleasing symmetry reflected the sunshine and cloudless sky, lending a come-hither look to the property.

They stepped out of the trees into a manicured swath of lawn.

Pam gasped and Steve grinned. The new owners had added onto the property, but the generous old home he remembered so fondly still stood.

A long, one-story enclosed porch ran the entire width of the home. Floor-to-ceiling windows looked out onto a flagstone patio crisscrossed with strings of party lights. An outdoor kitchen was located at one end of the patio. A large shed stood at a distance. Its double doors were open, revealing rolling carts full of round tables and banquet chairs.

"It's a wedding venue, all right." Pam pointed to a lattice canopy at the far side of the lawn.

"Okay—we've seen it. We'd better go back."

Pam and Chance walked slowly forward, examining everything in front of them.

Steve sighed in exasperation and followed them. "What're you doing? We shouldn't be creeping around here."

"We're not creeping." Pam didn't stop her forward progress. "We're simply looking. No harm in that." She walked across the patio and peered inside the porch. "That's a dance floor."

She made her way around the side of the house. "Look at this stonework," she said, running her hand along it. "I'd love to see this from the inside."

"We are not breaking in!"

She looked over her shoulder at him and rolled her eyes. "'Course not. But if we can see it from a front window? Well …"

She continued walking and mounted the steps to the porch. Picture windows on either side of the front door beckoned. Pam moved from one to the other, cupping her face with her hands and pressing her nose to the glass.

Steve hung back, alert for any signs that they were not alone on the property.

"This place is glorious," Pam said. "Don't you want to look?"

"I remember it from my childhood," Steve said. "I think we've taken our exploring a little too far."

"I've seen all I can," she said. "Unless it's unlocked, and we go inside." She reached for the door handle.

"No way!"

Pam giggled. "I'm just kidding. Even I wouldn't go that far." She crossed the porch to him and kissed him lightly. "Thanks for being a good sport. I know this has made you uncomfortable. Let's go."

Steve patted his thigh to call Chance to him. The dog fell into step with them, his wanderlust satisfied for the moment.

The three adventurers returned to the opening in the fence. Steve climbed over it while Pam and Chance squeezed through the gap. They crossed into the field without detection.

"I love that place," Pam said as they strolled back to their picnic, Chance trotting at their side. "Enchanted Grove Estate. Aptly named. I hope I get to attend a wedding there some day. I'll stick my nose into every room that isn't locked or barricaded. No one could stop me."

Steve grabbed her hand and brought it to his lips.

If he was successful that afternoon, her wish could come true in short order.

CHAPTER 8

"Where did you find all this yummy stuff?" Pam smeared a cracker with brie, topped it with fig jam, and popped it into her mouth, licking a dollop of jam off of her finger.

"I went to that bougie grocery on the road to Hartford."

"Terrific selections," she said, holding her hand to cover her mouth while she spoke. "That white cheddar is out of this world, too. I didn't realize how hungry I was. She picked up a slice of peppered salami. May I?" She gestured to Chance.

The dog sat at attention on the grass at the edge of their blanket. His mouth was open, and saliva dripped to the ground. His eyes remained locked on the food.

"He's not supposed to have it." Steve looked at his beloved dog. "But just this once won't hurt."

Pam turned to Chance and offered the rolled piece of meat to him.

Chance snatched and swallowed it before she had time to call his name.

"I almost forgot," Pam said, flipping onto her knees and crawling to the container of cookies. "We've got these." She popped off the plastic lid. "If you're too full to eat one right now, that's fine. I certainly am. I just wanted to show them to you because Mom and I decorated them last night."

Steve peered into the container, then laughed. "Are these what I think they are?"

"If that's good-luck St. Patrick's Day trolls, then you are correct."

"These are really cute. Here's another hidden talent I never knew you had." He reached his hand toward the container. "May I?"

"Of course. Pick whichever one you want."

Steve studied the cookies for a long moment.

"They all taste the same," Pam said. "The differences between the cookies are purely cosmetic."

Steve pursed his lips. One of these cookies might be his good luck charm. He glanced up at Pam, then selected a cookie.

"That's the one I thought you'd pick," she said

gleefully. "He's got polka dots on his shirt, and I know you like them."

"You're sure you don't mind if I eat this one?"

"Go for it. I want you to." Pam smiled. "The approved method of eating a troll cookie is to start at the top of the hat."

Steve rolled his eyes. "That's obvious. It's like starting with the ears on a chocolate bunny."

"Precisely."

Steve took a bite and moaned. "This may be the best cookie I've ever eaten."

"Mom baked them. It's her grandmother's recipe. I've loved them my whole life."

Steve finished the cookie, then got to his feet. "Can we leave this for a moment?" He offered her his hand.

She took it, and he pulled her to her feet.

"I think it's time we strolled through those wild-flowers."

"That's a great idea! I'd like to pick some to bring home."

Steve tucked her hand into his elbow and led her to the spot in the carpet of yellow and white flowers, where the blooms were tall and densely packed.

The sun shone, butterflies flitted, and a light breeze caused the blossoms to sway seductively.

Pam inhaled deeply. "This could not be more perfect," she said.

"Actually, I hope it can be." Steve pulled the ring box out of his pocket and dropped to one knee.

Pam gasped and blinked away tears as the realization of what was about to happen washed over her.

Steve took her hands in his. "Pam Olson, you have surprised and delighted me every day that I've known you. Even today, I've learned more wonderful things. You are the kindest, most interesting, and creative person I've ever met. I love watching the world through your eyes."

A tear traced a course down her cheek and splashed on their clasped hands.

"I'm a better man since I've known you. You support and encourage me in everything I do. I can be myself around you and you love me for who I am."

Pam squeezed his hand.

"I can't imagine a life without you. Together, I know we will rejoice in all the joys of life and take solace in each other during hard times. It would be the greatest honor of my life to travel this journey with you." He released one of her hands and fumbled with the ring box, flipping it open. "Will you do me the honor of marrying me?"

Pam sank to her knees and pulled him to her. Tears were now coming so fast she could barely talk. "Yes … yes … yes, I'll marry you."

Steve gently wiped the tears from her cheeks with his fingers, then leaned in to kiss her. Oblivious to the world around them, they lost themselves in a kiss that conveyed a connection that words could not.

Chance pranced around them. His sniffing and pawing went unnoticed. He finally wedged his muzzle between them and uttered a muted "Woof."

Pam was the first to draw back. She threw an arm around Chance's neck and drew him into a group hug. "Are you willing to share your daddy with me? I guess I'll become your dog mommy."

Chance wagged his tail so hard he almost fell over.

Steve laughed. "I think that's a yes."

The dog barked, running back to the blanket, settling himself down, the happy—now engaged—couple following.

"Okay, boy. Settle down." Steve moved the big dog to the edge of the blanket and commanded him to stay.

Chance reluctantly obeyed.

"Do you like the ring?" Steve asked. "Because—if you don't—we can exchange it."

"The ring! OMG—I was crying so hard, I couldn't see it."

Steve held up the open ring box.

Pam gasped and started to cry again. Her left hand shook as he slid the ring on her finger.

"Well?"

"I couldn't love it any more. It's my dream ring." She choked out the words. "And it fits perfectly." She reluctantly tore her eyes from her ring finger to look at him. "How did you know? This can't be a coincidence."

"I have to admit; Irene helped me with the selection of the ring."

"She knew about this?" Pam brought her hand to the side of her head. "Did she know you were going to propose today?"

Steve nodded.

"That little stinker! I was with her all day yesterday and she never let on."

"Irene promised me she'd keep my secret. She's the best."

Pam twisted her hand this way and that in the sunshine. "It looks like an updated version of my grandmother's ring—except the main diamond is way bigger."

"Irene knew you always loved that ring, so she let me take it to the jeweler on the square. I told them I wanted a larger central stone, but it needed to be styled like the ring I brought in."

"They nailed it. It's perfect."

"Irene took a ring from your jewelry drawer—one she knew you rarely wear—brought it to the jeweler to confirm the size, and snuck it back into your jewelry box." He sat forward on his haunches. "Did you ever notice it was missing?"

Pam shook her head. "You know me. I rarely wear jewelry and don't go into my jewelry box very often. That's going to change with this," she said, undulating her fingers. "I'm never taking this off."

She leaned into him. "Thank you, my love. I adore you and cannot wait to be your wife."

The world receded as they lost themselves in another kiss. When they came up for air, Steve stood and pulled her to her feet.

"I've got champagne. And real glass flutes. Shall we toast the moment?"

Pam put her right hand into his left one and allowed herself to be pulled back to their hamper, all the while admiring her ring.

"Do you mind if we wait until we're back in town? If we open it out here, we'll each have one glass before we pour the rest out. We can't have an open bottle in the car. If I know you, you've bought something very expensive."

"It's a special occasion. It doesn't matter."

"Let's stop at your sister's on the way home," Pam said. "I can't wait to tell them, and I'd like to show her my ring. We can share the champagne with Carol and Tom."

"That's a great idea."

"And we need to go see my mom, especially since she was in on all this." Pam drew a circle in the air around their picnic spot. "I want to tell her in person —today—and show her the ring. Has she seen it?"

"No. I picked it up from the jeweler yesterday. I had planned to propose at the end of the month at that fancy place you've been yearning to try."

"The one where it takes six months to get a reservation?"

"Yep. We'll still go there one of these days, but, with filming of season two starting next week, I decided to move everything up. We're both going to be run off our feet once that starts, and I wanted us to relax and enjoy this day."

They began stowing the picnic items into the hamper. "As lovely as I'm sure that restaurant is, it couldn't compete with all this." She stood and surveyed the scene behind them.

"I know what a romantic you are. Did this live up to your Hallmark Channel-fueled expectations?"

"No."

His face fell.

"It far exceeded them." She helped him fold the blanket. "You know what else? I think we found our wedding venue today."

"Enchanted Grove Estate?"

"Exactly. What do you think? I love it. We could search forever and not find anything better."

"I was hoping you'd say that."

She snapped the leash on Chance and picked up the cookies. Steve gathered the hamper and blanket and they set off for his SUV.

"When would you like to get married?" he asked. "What kind of wedding do you want?"

"Something small. Family and close friends. I've always wanted a fall wedding. Pumpkins, changing leaves, warm colors. Cozy."

"That sounds like you. It suits me just fine, too. How about this fall? I don't want to wait."

"Filming is supposed to finish by October 5. They've set the ribbon cutting of the new shelter for October 12."

"How about the week after that? With any luck, the leaves will be at their peak, and we won't have snow."

"I love that!" She clapped her hands together. "Look at us. We're engaged, we've found a venue, and have a wedding date in mind."

"Now we have to find out if Enchanted Grove Estate is available."

"I'll check their website on my phone while you drive us back to town. Things are coming together. I feel like good luck is surrounding us."

"Maybe it was that troll cookie, after all," Steve said.

"If that's the case, I'm going to get Mom's recipe and make sure we've always got them on hand."

CHAPTER 9

*P*am hunched over her phone as she scrolled and swiped. "The photos on their website are gorgeous. Enchanted Grove Estate is definitely where I want to get married." She tapped at the screen. "I hope they're not all booked up." She scrolled some more.

"Steve!" Her voice rose an octave. "You won't believe this."

He glanced away from the road in front of him.

Her eyes were shining.

"What?"

"The only Saturday that's still open—for the rest of the year—is October 19."

"You're kidding."

She shook her head. "It's meant to be."

"Better reserve the date."

"It says we have to meet with them in person to confirm a reservation." She scrolled and continued reading. "We can put down a $500 deposit to hold the date. The basic cost for the venue is $15,000." She brought her phone to her lap and sighed heavily.

Steve took his right hand off the steering wheel and fished his wallet out of his pocket. "Put it on my credit card," he said, passing the wallet to her.

"Really? That's not too much? We'll have to pay extra for food and beverages. Plus a photographer, videographer, flowers, and a disc jockey."

"I know what goes into a wedding." He smiled across at her.

"I thought you'd have a fit."

"I've got savings. We deserve the wedding we want."

"I'm so glad you feel that way." She opened his wallet and removed a credit card, holding it out to him. "This one?"

"Yep."

"I can contribute, too," she said, entering the credit card details on the website's reservation form. Pam tapped at the screen with a flourish. "There." She paused, her lips moving as she silently read the message on the screen. "We've reserved the date and someone from the venue will contact me on Tuesday to set up a meeting with us."

Steve pulled her hand to his lips and kissed it. "October 19. I like it."

"Me too. I hope the other arrangements come together as smoothly." She pressed back into her seat. "The last time we did the TV series, I was overbooked with just my day job and filming. I don't know how I'm going to also plan a wedding—especially one this fast."

"I don't want you to stress out about this. We can always go to the courthouse to get married."

"No. I want a proper wedding."

"I was going to say that I'll help—and I will—but we both know I'm not good with this sort of thing." He pursed his lips, thinking. "What about a wedding planner?"

"That's an added expense, but we may have to consider using one."

"I say we do it."

"I'll ask around to see if I can find one," Pam said. She brought her hand to her mouth to cover a yawn, even though it was only 4:00.

"We've gotten engaged, set the date, and reserved the wedding venue. I think that's enough for one day," Steve said. "Except telling our families. If you're not too beat, we'll stop by your mom's and then my sister's to share the news."

"Will your parents be there for Sunday dinner?"

"Yep. We'll get both of our families told and then we'll call it quits."

"Sounds good to me," Pam said, powering down her window an inch to allow the breeze to revive her.

Their first stop was Irene's home. Pam's mother had established a beachhead on her front porch, with her knitting, her book club book, the Sunday paper, and a large tumbler of iced tea. She was ensconced on the wicker settee that lived on her porch from spring through fall.

They pulled to the curb in front of the quaint bungalow, and Irene tossed her knitting aside and walked to the top of the steps to greet them.

Pam leapt out of the car and raced to her mother's open arms. "You stinker," she said, pulling her mother close and holding her tight. "You knew."

Irene shrugged. "Some secrets are not mine to tell." She took Pam's face in her hands and looked into her daughter's eyes. "That's what I love to see," she whispered, pulling her back into their hug. "You said yes!"

Pam nodded her head against her mother's shoulders.

Irene looked up to see Steve lingering on the walkway, giving the mother and daughter a private moment. She extended her arm to him. "Get over here," she commanded.

He did as directed and stepped into a group hug.

Irene leaned across and kissed his cheek. "I'm thrilled you're going to be my son-in-law. I already love you like you're one of my own."

"Ditto, Irene," he said.

"Let's see that ring." Irene stepped back. "Did it fit?"

Pam extended her left hand to Irene. "Perfectly. I love it so much."

"Ohhh … I can see why. It's stunning."

"Thanks for guiding Steve in the right direction."

"I know how much you love your grandmother's ring. I must say—that enormous diamond makes it so much prettier." She looked at Steve. "You've done very well."

Steve flushed with pride. "We've set the date and found the venue," he blurted out, diverting attention from the ring.

"Wow—already?"

"October 19 at Enchanted Grove Estate."

"On the outskirts of town?"

Pam nodded.

"That's lovely. How did you know about it?"

Pam yawned again. "That's a story for another

time. I'll call you tomorrow. Right now, we want to stop by to share our news with Steve's family."

"Carol and my parents will skin me alive if they hear about this on the grapevine," Steve said.

"And I want to show them all my ring!"

"As you should. Thank you for stopping to see me. I was hoping you would," she said sheepishly.

"Looks like you were camped out, waiting for us."

Irene chuckled. "Guilty as charged. Now—go share your good news. And call me tomorrow. I want to hear all the details."

Irene swept them into a group hug again, then watched them walk back to Steve's SUV.

Steve's phone chirped with an incoming text as they were buckling their seatbelts. "It's from Carol," he said. "While you and your mom were having a moment, I texted her to tell her we were going to stop by for a few minutes."

His brow furrowed as he read the text. "She says that we are to stay as far away from them as humanly possible. The kids traded colds all week long and are still coughing and sneezing. Carol came down with it yesterday and Tom just told her he has a temperature. Mom and Dad canceled dinner late last week because Dad had started with the sniffles."

"Oh, no. I'm so sorry to hear this."

"I'll text them our news."

Pam put her hand out to stop him. "Don't do that. Wouldn't you like to tell your family in person?"

"Yes, but how will that work? Nobody in this town can keep a secret," Steve said.

"We won't tell anybody else until we've seen your family. I'll text my mom to let her know not to talk about it."

"We know she's good at keeping secrets," Steve said. He touched the ring. "You won't be able to wear that."

"That'll be hard, but it won't be for long. I'll put it on this chain with the locket my dad gave me when I turned sixteen. I always wear that. No one will notice."

Steve caressed her face with the palm of his hand. "That's incredibly thoughtful." He leaned over to kiss her as she yawned again.

"I think someone needs to go straight home."

"I don't know what's gotten into me. All the sunshine, I guess." She pulled him to her for a kiss. "Don't take all the yawning the wrong way. This has been the best, most exciting day of my life."

CHAPTER 10

The rumble of voices filled the room. People milled about, falling into small groups for congenial conversation. Some gathered at architectural plans or aerial photos taped to the walls, examining and pointing.

Pam and Steve stood near a podium at one end of the room. Jed Duncan stood at their side.

Laura and her mother sat in the first row of chairs, directly across from Pam. The girl crossed her ankles and swung her feet under the chair, her hands clasped tightly in her lap.

Pam greeted the pair. "I'm so glad you're here." She squatted so she was at eye level with the girl. "We want to recognize you for coming up with the project for season two. The entire community is excited about it."

Laura twisted her hands and swung her feet even faster.

"She's anxious," Laura's mother said. "About being on TV."

"I understand that." Pam smiled into the girl's eyes. "The same thing happens to me right before we begin filming. My mouth gets dry, and I forget what I want to say."

Laura nodded vigorously.

"Once we start, all that goes away. You'll see."

Laura slowed her fidgeting.

"Steve is going to thank you for coming up with the idea for the shelter and ask you to stand up and wave to the crowd. That's all. You don't have to say a word."

A hint of a smile played at Laura's lips.

"Your mom is right here, too. Would you like her to stand up with you?"

Laura nodded yes. She then pointed to Pam.

Pam touched the base of her neck. "You want me to stand with you, too?"

Again, Laura nodded.

"Then that's what we'll do." Pam looked at Laura's mother. "When Steve acknowledges you, we'll both be at your side."

Marty Beckman walked to the podium.

Pam stepped back into place.

"Our crew is ready to film," Marty said. "We plan to use only a minute of footage from this organizational meeting of construction volunteers. We won't yell 'cut' or do retakes. Just keep the meeting going as you've planned, and we'll get what we need."

"Okay." Pam shifted her weight from foot to foot.

"You aren't nervous, are you?" Marty asked. "This is season two. You're an old pro at this."

She forced a smile as she remembered the words of encouragement she'd just given Laura. "I'm fine when I'm doing something and I don't know the camera is there. Standing up here—in front of everybody and talking? Not my thing."

Steve rested his hand lightly on her back. "You know everyone in here, don't you?"

Pam studied the crowd in front of her, then nodded.

"We're just talking to friends," he said.

"When you put it like that, it seems less scary."

"You'll be great," Marty said. He looked at Steve. "Time to call the meeting to order."

Steve nodded and stepped to the microphone as Marty joined the film crew stationed on one side of the room. He tapped the microphone, triggering a magnified thumping sound that silenced conversations. Groups broke apart as people took their seats.

"Welcome. What a terrific turnout for this organizational meeting of volunteer workers to build a no-kill animal shelter in Linden Falls."

A smattering of applause ran around the room.

"The idea for the shelter came from Laura Thompson, and she and her mother are here with us tonight. I'd like to invite her to stand so we can recognize her for her contribution."

Laura's mother stood and took Laura's hand, pulling her to her feet.

Pam quickly moved to the girl and turned her to face the audience.

Jed began to clap, and the others in the room followed suit with a reception any politician would envy.

Laura's skin turned pink from her collar to the tip of her head. She brought her right hand up to chin level and gave a shy wave to the crowd of Linden Falls locals, who only clapped louder.

"Well done," Pam whispered in Laura's ear as Laura and her mother resumed their seats, and she stepped back to the podium.

"I want to thank Linden Falls Fitness for allowing us to hold our organizational meeting here." Steve looked across the sea of faces in front of him. "I know many of you are regulars here. For those of you who've never been inside, Pam and I will give a tour of the facilities to anyone who wants one." He swung his head sharply to look at Jed, eyeing him—with a smirk—from head to toe.

The crowd laughed.

Jed grinned. "Point made." He patted his small paunch. "I'll take that tour."

"I also want to thank Duncan's Hardware for donating the building and land where the shelter will be located. He told me not to make a big deal of it." Steve turned again to Jed, who shrugged and looked at the floor. "That donation—together with volunteer labor from all of you—will allow us to open the shelter this fall."

The room erupted into another round of applause.

Steve waited for the noise to die down. "Terry Grant has agreed to act as the general contractor on the project. We'll work under his license, and he'll pull the permits." He motioned for a stocky man with a shock of white hair and a Santa Claus-worthy beard to come to the microphone. "Tell us how you're going to organize this project."

Terry walked to the front of the room. "I've worked with every single volunteer in this room during my thirty-plus years in construction in this area. You're all the best of the best." He pointed to the back row. "I see a handful of you are even coming out of retirement to help. I'm delighted to see that.

We've got sign-up sheets posted by the register at Duncan's for the team you want to work on. You've got your choice of plumbing, electrical, framing, drywall, finish carpentry, painting, and flooring." He leaned across the podium and swung his gaze around the room. "Some of you can do all of them, so don't be shy about signing up for more than one."

A titter of laughter ran around the room.

"We're planning to work only on the weekends, unless crews are available to work during the week. I know this seems like an impossible timeline, but a lot of the infrastructure is already in place. Barb McVey," he scanned the audience until he located the older woman with graying blonde hair seated in the middle, "please stand. Barb's offered to update and post work schedules. We'll send them out via email, put them on the Duncan's Hardware website, and, for those of you who are old school, they'll be posted by the register at Duncan's."

A hand shot up in the middle of the room.

Terry smiled. "I believe Neva Cabot has something she wants to say."

Neva leapt to her feet. "You know I'm not volunteering to do construction, but I can feed the workers—and organize others to provide snacks and such."

"That's really nice," Terry began.

Neva waved her hand to silence him. "It's not just The Wishing Tree Inn that will contribute, either. Cobblestone Deli & Bakery, Crooked Porch Cafe, Doc's Fountain, and Woody's Pizza have all offered to provide food."

The crowd erupted in applause.

Neva flushed with pleasure at the reaction.

"We'll all need gym memberships to work off the extra pounds we'll put on during construction," someone quipped.

Neva chuckled. "I've started a sign-up sheet." She looked across the room at Barb. "I'll keep you updated, and I'll post at Duncan's, too."

Barb nodded at her, and Neva sat back down.

Terry extended his arm to Jed. "I'd like Jed to tell us about the property."

Jed moved forward. "My grandfather built the building as a warehouse for the hardware store, and it served us well until we outgrew it and built a new one five years ago. It was never open to the public, so you might not know about it. We've maintained it well. I put a new roof on it four years ago. It already has functional restrooms, and we replaced the heating and cooling systems the year before last. I always thought I would sell the place—and I've had offers to buy it—but nothing felt right for Linden Falls. I'm glad I hung onto it."

He took a deep breath. All eyes in the room were fixed on him. "Some of you knew my grandfather."

Many in the audience nodded.

"He loved his family, his hardware store, and animals. There were always dogs and cats at my grandparents' house. He'd bring home any stray he came across. I remember one time when I was about ten. He pulled his truck off the side of the road because he thought he saw a dog in the tree line. He was right, and that dog became my best friend."

Jed's voice caught in his throat. "My grandfather would be thrilled to see his warehouse, the building he was so proud of, serving as a shelter."

The crowd rose to their feet and clapped.

Jed motioned for them to sit. "With the expertise in this room, I know we can make the necessary changes in no time."

"Darn right!" someone called from the back of the room.

"We'll begin with a small amount of demo. We'll have plans and permits this week." Jed stepped aside and let Steve return to the podium.

"Filming starts the last weekend of this month. If you haven't already signed release forms with the production company, please see Marty in the back of the room." Steve reached over and pulled a surprised-looking Pam to the microphone. "And now—for the news you've all been waiting for." He bent and whispered in her ear.

Pam leaned toward the microphone. "Ribbon cutting will be October 12!"

People jumped to their feet amidst applause and cheering.

Pam and Steve smiled into each other's eyes.

CHAPTER 11

*P*am slipped into her jacket, hoisted her purse onto her shoulder, and walked out of the trainer's break room at Linden Falls Fitness. Tuesday was her early day, with her last training session ending at 4:30. The frozen meal she planned to microwave for her dinner wasn't too appealing, but the prospect of a long bath and early night certainly was.

Steve didn't finish his workday until 8:30. He'd call her from the car on his way home and she'd head to bed as soon as they hung up.

She was about to reach for the push bar on the double glass entry doors when she heard him call her name. Pam turned and smiled as Steve hurried toward her.

"I'm glad I caught you," he said. He opened the door for her and stepped outside after her.

"Don't you have a client right now?"

He shook his head. "Three of my Tuesday night regulars are out of town, and the other one just called in sick. As of right now, I'm done for the day."

"I'm sorry about the one who is sick, but it's always nice to have a night off. I'd offer to make you dinner, but I didn't make it to the grocery this week. All I've got to offer are TV dinners from the freezer."

"That's the other great news: everyone in my family is well now. Carol just invited us to dinner at their house. It's Tom's week off from the hospital and he's made lasagna and a homemade sourdough loaf. Mom and Dad will be there, too."

"We can tell them our good news!" Her hand instantly flew to her ring, hanging on the chain with her locket.

"Exactly. I want them to know; I want everyone in this town to know!" He pulled her into his arms and kissed her.

Pam took a step back and wriggled out of his arms. "Not here," she admonished him. "We're in front of the place where we both work. What will people think?"

"They'll be happy to see it. Everyone loves

romance." He took her hand and turned them toward the parking lot.

Barb and Brian McVey approached on their way into the gym. Barb grinned at them and Brian gave a thumbs up.

"There you go," Steve said. "They saw us kissing and they're in favor of it."

Pam chuckled. "Maybe so, but let's keep the public displays of affection to a minimum."

"Party pooper," Steve teased. "I need to head home to give Chance his dinner and let him out."

"I should feed Leopold."

"We'll take care of our pets and I'll pick you up. We can be at Carol's in half an hour."

"Okay." Pam reached up and removed the hair tie corralling her ponytail. Thick auburn plaits tumbled to her shoulders. She finger-combed her unruly hair as they walked to her SUV.

Steve took her hands in his and brought them gently to her sides. "You look stunning. Don't go into a mad dash fussing with your hair and makeup as soon as you get home."

"I want to look presentable for your family when we tell them—not like I've been working out for hours and need a shower," she said.

Steve cut her off. "My family adores you." He

leaned into her and sniffed along her neck. "No worries—you smell great."

Pam rolled her eyes. "Take your time with Chance. I'm going to spin through the shower, change clothes, and run a curling iron through my hair."

"Nothing I say will change your mind, will it?"

Pam shook her head.

"How much time do you need?"

"Twenty minutes? I'll be super-fast." Pam unlocked her car and flung herself behind the wheel.

"You've got it. I'll text Carol that we'll be there by 5:30."

Pam smiled up at him as she started her car. "That's plenty of time. Thank you!"

Steve stepped aside as she headed for home. Forty-five minutes later, he knocked on her front door.

Pam ripped the curling iron's cord out of the socket, tousled her hair into place, and went over it with a light mist of hair spray. She swiped over her lips with lip gloss, slipped her feet into a pair of heeled sandals, and smoothed the front of her sapphire blue sheath.

Steve knocked on her door again.

Pam gave Leopold a quick pat as she snatched her clutch from her bed. "Sorry we didn't have time for a snuggle," she said to her beloved cat. "Mommy's got to go out."

She hurried to the door and opened it as Steve prepared to knock again.

"Oh … wow," he said, stepping back to look her up and down. "You're gorgeous."

Pam turned in a circle. "Did I clean up all right?"

"You look like you're ready for a night on the town."

Pam's face fell. "Oh, gosh. Is this too much? Should I change?"

"It's me who should change. I'm wearing the clothes I put on this morning. Are you sure you want to be seen with me?"

"You're fine," Pam said. "It's just … I want to look pretty when they learn I'm joining the family."

"Pretty isn't the half of it." He held out his arm to her. "Let's go. I'm excited to tell them our news."

Leopold meowed from inside the doorway.

Steve reached behind Pam to give the cat a quick scratch between the ears. "Sorry, boy. You have to share her with me tonight."

"Mommy will be back," Pam cooed to the cat as she shut the door.

Steve leaned toward her for a kiss and she quickly turned her cheek to him.

"Lipstick," they both said in unison.

"I promise not to muss up anything on the way to Carol's," Steve said, "but, when I bring you home, all bets are off."

Pam cuffed his shoulder.

"Where's the ring?"

She held up her hand, and the stones sparkled under the porch light.

"Good. I want everyone to see it there. Let's go!"

CHAPTER 12

Steve pulled into his sister's driveway just after 5:30.

Ben, his thirteen-year-old nephew, jumped to his feet from the bottom step of the porch. "They're here," he called over his shoulder.

His younger brother, Riley, opened the door into the house and relayed the message.

Carol stepped onto the porch, drying her hands on a towel. "You two go inside and wash your hands," she said to the boys. "Tell the others we're ready to eat. Gramma and Grampa serve themselves first."

Ben trotted up the steps. "We know, Mom. Company always goes first."

"Exactly." Carol gave him a fond pat on the back as he passed her, heading into the house.

"I'm glad you could join us on such short notice." Carol accepted a kiss on the cheek from her brother and leaned in to hug Pam.

"We're excited to be here," Steve said. "We want to talk to you."

"Do you mind if we sit down to eat first?" Carol asked. "We can talk after dinner. Tom's lasagna smells so good. We've all been salivating for the past hour. I didn't let the kids load up on after-school snacks, and they're starving."

"I skipped lunch," Pam said, "so I'm good with that."

"I can always eat," Steve said. He glanced at Pam and she gave him a reassuring nod.

"Right this way. We're serving buffet style on the kitchen island. Get your food and head for the dining room."

Pam and Steve joined the hubbub in the kitchen, Steve waving to his parents across the room. Lori and Dave Turner nodded to them as they moved to the dining room with their loaded plates.

Ben and Riley hovered near the food, waiting for Pam and Steve to serve themselves.

"Your grandmother made me wait until everyone else took what they wanted. I guess it's the fate of being a hungry boy," Steve said, sliding a large slice of lasagna onto his plate. "I think you can help your-selves now."

The boys sprang into action. Dave said the blessing the second everyone was seated. Cutlery clicked against plates as the family tucked into the delicious meal.

"This is delicious, Tom," Pam said. "Is this an old family recipe, with sauce that's been simmering on the stove all day?"

"Afraid not, but I'm happy you think it might be. I used sauce from a jar and doctored it up with fresh herbs."

"I'm glad to hear it," she said, covering her mouth with her left hand. "Maybe you can give me some pointers."

"I'd be—," he began, when nine-year-old Emma interrupted him.

She jumped out of her chair and extended her arm across the table, pointing at Pam. "Look!" she cried. "It's making rainbows on the tablecloth."

All eyes turned to Pam. Her engagement ring sparkled in a swath of light from the chandelier.

"Is that what I think it is?" Carol asked, pushing back her chair and getting to her feet.

Pam flushed.

"It is," Steve said. "That's what we wanted to tell you. Pam and I are engaged."

Lori brought her hand to her heart. "My prayers have been answered." She glanced at her husband. "We've both been hoping for this." She fumbled in her pocket for a tissue and dabbed at her eyes.

"Congratulations, son," Dave said. "And welcome to the family, Pam. You've felt like the one for him since the moment we met you."

Carol walked around the table and bent to hug Steve and then Pam. "We all agree. When the two of you took that ridiculous 'no dating' pledge, I thought this day might never come. It's been obvious to everyone who knows you that you're perfect together." Her voice caught in her throat. "I'm thrilled you've finally realized it."

"Can I see your ring?" Emma asked.

Pam got out of her chair and walked around the table, allowing everyone to take a close look.

"That's absolutely stunning," Lori said. "It's not vintage, but it's got a certain nostalgic look about it."

Carol held Pam's hand as she studied the ring. "Well said, Mom. Did you pick it out together?"

Pam shook her head. "Steve collaborated with my mother on it. She knew I've always loved my grandmother's ring. He took that ring to the jeweler on the square and they made this."

"Are you pleased with it?" Carol asked.

"I couldn't love anything more."

Carol pulled Pam in for another hug. "I'm so glad." She looked at Steve. "Nicely done, bro."

Pam sat down again and resumed eating.

"Have you set a date?" Tom asked.

Steve filled them in on the few details they'd settled on.

"Fall weddings are my favorite," Lori said.

"Will you have a beautiful dress?" Emma asked. "Like a big princess one?"

Pam smiled at the little girl. "I'm not sure. My style is more casual and tailored, but I've wanted a ball gown since I was your age."

"With a giant floofy skirt," Emma supplied.

"The problem is, I don't have enough time before the wedding to order a dress. I'll probably go to a bridal boutique and buy whatever sample dress fits me." She put her hand to her head. "With the filming of season two starting next weekend, I'm not sure how I'm going to get everything done."

"We're going to hire a wedding planner, remember?" Steve rubbed her back gently. "That'll help tremendously."

Carol spoke to Ben. "Please go get the wedding photo on the bookcase by the piano."

"The one of you and Dad?"

She nodded.

Ben soon returned with the framed picture of

Tom in his tuxedo and Carol in her lace wedding gown. He handed it to his mother.

"Thank you, sweetheart," she said, allowing her gaze to linger on the photo before she handed it across the table to Pam.

"This was my dream gown."

Lori's eyes shown as she spoke. "Miles of lace, tulle, sequins, and seed pearls."

"I'll never forget how beautiful you looked as you stood at the end of the aisle, on your father's arm," Tom said.

"Mom had a princess dress," Emma said. "That's what I'll want when I get married."

Pam bent over the photo. "It's a glorious dress. You look incredible." She brought her head up. "Both of you. Did you have to order it?"

Carol nodded. "It took almost a year. We got worried we wouldn't receive it in time. Do you remember that, Mom?"

"Of course. I marched into the boutique one afternoon and raised a ruckus. I think that helped."

Pam looked at the dress again. "I'd adore something like this." She handed the photo back to Carol.

Riley leaned forward, his elbows on the table. "Are we having dessert?"

"As soon as you boys clear the table," Tom said, getting out of his chair.

Ben and Riley sprang into action. Steve joined them.

"I wouldn't ask this in front of Steve, since grooms aren't supposed to know about the dress," Carol said, "but would you like to wear mine? We're the same height and I was slimmer back then. I think it would fit you."

Pam gasped and stared at Carol.

"If you don't want to, my feelings won't be hurt. Don't hesitate to say no."

"Are you kidding me? If your dress fits, I'd be honored to wear it."

"It's in a big box on the top shelf of my closet. When would you like to try it on?"

"I'm taking a day off a week from Thursday to tour the venue. My appointment is at 10:00. Could I come by after that?"

"Perfect. I'll fix us lunch and you can tell me all about your visit."

"Would you mind if my mother came, too? I know she'll want to see it." Pam turned to Lori. "Would you like to be there, too?"

Lori put her hand on her heart. "Thank you for including me. I'd love that."

"It's a plan, then. This is so exciting," Carol said.

Ben and Riley reentered the dining room, each carrying a plate of brownies.

Steve and Tom followed with steaming cups of coffee.

"What have you cooked up while we were gone?" Tom asked. "If I know my wife, she's planning your engagement party."

Carol's head snapped up. "OMG—yes!"

"With our work and filming schedules, I don't think we'll have a spare evening for one," Steve said.

"Steve's right, I'm afraid. We don't want you to go to any trouble. This lunch on Thursday is enough."

Carol blew across her coffee. Her eyes suddenly expanded as she stared at Pam and Steve across the table. "I've got it. *I'll* be your wedding planner!"

"Oh, gosh," Pam stammered. "That's a huge job."

"This sort of thing is my strong suit," Carol said, her words coming fast. "And I won't push my ideas on you. You'll make all the decisions and my job will be to bring you options to review. I'll handle all the details."

Steve turned to face Pam. "Carol would be great at it."

"Discuss it—think about it—I don't want to push you."

"It's not that," Pam said, "but you've got your own job and the kids … it's a lot to ask."

"You're not asking. I'm offering. If I can't throw you an engagement party—and you probably won't have time for a shower, either—at least let me do this for you."

Lori spoke up. "She means it, dear. Do what you feel is best, but don't turn Carol down because you'd be imposing."

Carol brought her clasped hands to her chest and looked from Pam to Steve and back again.

Pam burst out laughing. "If you're really sure about this, then yes. I have confidence in you and your judgment. I know I'd be in excellent hands with you."

Carol sprang from her chair and ran around the table to sweep Pam into a hug. "This is going to be so much fun."

Pam hugged her back. "We'll get to know each other really well. I like that."

"Me too. Everything is going to be perfect for your wedding. I promise!"

CHAPTER 13

*J*ed watched Neva Cabot glide toward him across the lobby of The Wishing Tree Inn. Her long, loose skirt swirled around her ankles and her thick, white hair cascaded past her shoulders, reminding him of a Maltese he'd seen in a dog show on television.

She welcomed him with open arms. "To what do I owe the pleasure of this weekday visit?"

The old friends hugged.

"I'm here for two reasons. First, I want to thank you for organizing the food donations for the construction crews at the shelter."

"It's the least I could do," Neva said, raising her hand in a dismissive gesture. "I'm excited about this project."

"Glad to hear it," Jed continued, "because I'm here to ask you for more help with it."

Neva raised a questioning eyebrow as the swinging door into the kitchen opened. A blast of fragrant steam enveloped the server bringing a plate of scones to the buffet in the tearoom.

It was Jed's turn to resemble a dog, as he sniffed the air. "Those smell amazing." His eyes followed the server.

"Today's featured scone is lemon poppyseed," Neva said. "They're my favorite. That's the first batch out of the oven."

Jed's mouth watered, and he swallowed hard.

Neva put her hand on his elbow. "Janie's out for the day, so let's talk in her office. I'll have tea and scones brought in for us."

"You don't have to do that. I wouldn't want to impose," Jed said. His words were polite, but his eyes were full of desire for those scones.

"Nonsense. I never let myself enjoy a cup of tea and a scone when I'm by myself. You'll be doing me a favor." She tucked her hand into his arm and led them down the hallway to her former—now Janie's—cozy office. She steered him to one of the wing-back chairs in front of the fireplace, tapped the intercom to request tea and scones from the kitchen, and joined him in the other chair.

Jed sat forward and rested his elbows on his knees. "This new shelter is becoming a bigger deal than I realized."

"Duncan's has been extraordinarily generous," Neva replied. "If you need to cut back, everyone will understand. It's a huge expense."

"It's not money." Jed was quick to respond. "In the short time since we announced the project, I've had dozens—probably hundreds—of calls or emails from people expressing interest and suggesting other uses for the property."

A light knock sounded on the partially open office door and a server entered, carrying a tray loaded with a pot of tea, two cups, a jar of honey, a pitcher of cream, and a plate of steaming scones.

Neva nodded at the round tea table next to her chair and the server deposited the tray on it. The woman lifted the lid on the pot of tea. "It's not ready yet," she said to Neva.

"Thank you. I'll let it steep and pour our cups myself."

With a nod and a smile, the woman left the room.

Neva handed Jed a small plate and offered him a scone.

He gratefully accepted one and took a bite. "This tastes even better than it smells." He set the scone on his plate and licked his fingers.

Neva served herself a scone. "Everyone in town is talking about the shelter. It seems people were eager for a cause to rally around. I think you've found it."

Jed tilted his head to one side. "That's a good way of putting it. This shelter means more to our community than I would have imagined. Based on the comments I've received, it could function as a community center."

"I can see that." Neva checked on the tea. Satisfied that it was ready to drink, she poured them each a cup. "Cream or honey?"

Jed shook his head no.

Neva handed him his cup and stirred a generous teaspoonful of lavender honey into hers.

"People have suggested we put in a dog park, a coffee shop, a bookstore, a grooming salon—and even a people salon. The list goes on and on. I've stopped keeping track."

"The ones that are dog—or cat—related are a natural fit," Neva said.

"That's what I thought. Like the dog park. There's ample room for one, and it would bring people to the property—people who might want to adopt another dog."

Neva nodded her agreement.

"As ideas kept rolling in, I realized I don't want to decide on my own. I'm an expert on hardware stores, not animal shelters. I need input from others on what our community wants out there." He took a sip of his tea and lowered his cup to his lap. He held her gaze. "No one knows this community better than you, Neva. You've got your finger on the pulse of this town. Always have."

Neva chuckled. "As Keeper of Wishes from our Wishing Tree, I guess I know a lot about what people in Linden Falls really want."

"It's not just that you take the wishes off the tree when it rains and put them back up," he replied forcefully. "It's who you are, as a person, Neva. You're the most empathetic person I've ever met."

Neva shrugged. "I know and care about the people in this town," she said modestly. "Linden Falls has been a wonderful place to live my life, and being a steward of those wishes has meant more than keeping pieces of paper dry. It's been a privilege to nurture other people's dreams."

"That's why you're the perfect person to ask— will you chair a community group to source, consider, and recommend additional uses for the shelter property?" He leaned imperceptibly closer to her.

She stared back at him.

"I know you're already extremely busy around here," he began before she cut him off.

"Since my niece has taken over the running of the inn, I'm more like a third wheel." She reached over and squeezed his hand. "Yes, Jed," she replied. "I'd love to do that. It would bring me joy."

Jed released the breath he didn't realize he'd been holding. "Thank you, Neva. I feel so much better. I've got my hands full with all the construction stuff and the television show. I'm also not as qualified to do the job."

"I think you sell yourself short," Neva said, giving his hand another squeeze before releasing it. "But I'm thrilled you asked me."

"How will you start?"

"I think I'll recruit a group from the community. I need time to think about it, but Irene Olson, your sister, and Laura Thompson need to be on my committee."

"I know Paige will say yes. She calls and texts me multiple times a day with ideas. Irene is always a good choice. But Laura? She's a kid."

"Yes—with a big heart and bigger ideas. If her mother approves—and I think she will—Laura will be a key contributor."

Jed broke off a piece of his scone. "I'm so glad I placed this in your hands. What about Pam or Steve?"

Neva pursed her lips as she thought. "They're too busy."

"With their full-time jobs and hosting *Wishes of Home*, I'll bet you're right."

"It's not just that," Neva said.

"Oh? Is something else going on with them?"

"I have a feeling about them. I don't know what it is yet, but Pam and Steve are extra busy."

"I trust your gut instincts, Neva."

They both took a bite of their scones and enjoyed their tea.

CHAPTER 14

"*T*here it is," Carol said, pointing to a large, white signboard bearing the name Enchanted Grove Estate in a fancy black script embellished with gold.

Pam turned off the highway onto a winding driveway leading through a tall stand of trees. As before, the house revealed itself in increments, until they cleared the overhang of trees. She stopped the car at the first unobstructed view. Both women sat in silence, taking in the sight before them.

Carol was the first to speak. "I remember this place from when I was a kid. Steve used to play here. I'd ride along with Mom or Dad when they dropped him off, just to see this."

"It's not ostentatious or overly grand," Pam said, "but it is lovely."

"The symmetry and the proportions are all very pleasing. I can see that now, as an adult." Carol glanced at Pam. "This is the perfect place to get married. Thank you so much for letting me come with you this morning."

"You're my wedding planner," Pam said. "You had to be here." She read the site map and directional sign to her left. "It tells us to go right for the event coordinator's office." She followed the arrows and parked in the lot indicated, close to a door marked with the words Events Administration.

"We're right on time," Carol said. "If we leave here by eleven-thirty, we can pick up our takeout order from the Crooked Porch Cafe and be at my house before our mothers arrive at noon."

"Our appointment and tour are scheduled for an hour, so that should work well."

The two women were walking toward the office when the door was opened by a woman in a simple black sheath, her dark hair sleeked back into a neat chignon. Vibrant pink lipstick enlarged the smile that radiated welcome.

"I saw you pull up," she said, extending her hand to Pam. "We spoke on the phone. My name is Nancy. I'll be your contact person here at Enchanted Grove Estate."

Pam shook her hand and introduced Carol.

"I'm glad you have a wedding planner. Things go so much smoother when couples don't do it all themselves." She motioned for them to follow her. "Let me take down the details, then I'll give you a tour."

Carol and Pam entered a tidy office. A computer keyboard and monitor were the only items on Nancy's mahogany desk. Behind her, a bookshelf held large, black three-ring binders labeled Ceremony, Reception, Music, Decor, and Food.

Carol and Pam sat in cushioned chairs across the desk from Nancy.

"Let's get started," Nancy said. "I'll ask you several questions. If you know the answer, that's great, but it's fine if you haven't decided about most of these things yet. You've got plenty of time before your wedding."

Pam talked while Nancy's fingers flew across her keyboard for the next thirty minutes. The wedding party would include the bride and groom, with Carol as the matron of honor and Pam's brother, Kurt, as best man.

"That's all?" Nancy asked.

Pam looked at Carol. "Would Emma like to be a flower girl? It seems to me like she would enjoy that."

"Honestly, she's been talking about nothing else."

"Why didn't you say something?"

"This is your wedding. You get to decide who's in it."

"Do the boys want to play a part in it? I wouldn't want to leave them out."

"No worries on that score. They're fine being in the audience."

"I'll have one flower girl," Pam told Nancy.

"I've got you down for thirty to forty people, including the wedding party. That gives us lots of flexibility in terms of where the ceremony can take place and the reception held. All of our areas accommodate that number."

Nancy scrolled down her screen. "You want a 4:30 ceremony, followed by passed hors d'oeuvres, a plated meal, pie—instead of wedding cake—and dancing?"

Pam and Carol nodded in unison.

"You're making this very easy." Nancy swiveled her chair to the bookcase behind her and pulled out the binder labeled Decor. "Here are photos of the decor we offer as part of your base price for the venue. You're welcome to bring in your own items, but it'll be at your expense, and you'll have to place it and remove it the day of the wedding." She opened the binder on her desk and flipped to the FALL tab.

Pam and Carol hunched over photos of wedding

arches, table settings, and floral arrangements, turning pages back and forth.

"I like this group," Pam said, tapping the clear page protector of a photo featuring pumpkins, mums, hydrangeas, and roses in shades of peach, orange, cream, blush, and mauve. "What do you think?" she asked Carol.

"Breathtaking. I'd choose them, too."

"That's my favorite fall grouping," Nancy said. "You won't be sorry." She removed a copy of the photo from the sleeve protector and handed it to Carol. "You can take this with you."

Carol pulled a pleated folio labeled Pam/Steve Wedding from her bag and slipped the photo inside.

"I love working with people who are so decisive," Nancy said. "I'll email both of you a checklist of items to consider as you plan your wedding and reception, together with our list of suggested vendors, and the dates when you need to send things to us. From what I've seen, the two of you won't have problems with any of it. We'll set up a food tasting in early fall. We use fresh, seasonal ingredients, so we have to wait until closer to the wedding to do that."

"That sounds great," Pam said. "Your first line of contact should be Carol."

"I figured as much," Nancy said. "You're about to

start filming the new season of *Wishes of Home*. You're going to be extremely busy."

"You know about our show?"

"I recorded the entire first season and have watched it several times." Her crisp demeanor softened. "I'm a big fan. Your wedding is right after season two ends, so I know you won't have time for all these wedding details."

"That's what I'm here for," Carol said. "The bride and groom will make all the decisions, but I'll handle communications."

Nancy smiled at them as she reshelved the binder and closed their file on her computer. "Would you like to tour the venue now?"

Pam and Carol leapt to their feet.

"We'll start at the parking lot, so you can get a feel for the flow of the spaces."

They were soon approaching the front of the house from the lot. Nancy took them to the side where the two-story stone fireplace dominated one wall. "This open area, here, is where we set up outdoor ceremonies. We arrange chairs in two sections with a central aisle for the bride to walk down. We put an arched trellis at that end so you'll be in front of the setting sun. Sunset is around six in October. If the weather is mild, an outdoor wedding will be spectacular."

"I'd love that," Pam said.

"If it's not, we can easily move you inside. I'll show you that space now. We've opened it up, so the former living and dining rooms are one large space."

Carol and Pam trailed after her into an open concept area with large, sashed windows, gleaming hardwood floors, and a massive stone fireplace with a carved mahogany mantel.

"This might be prettier than the outside area," Pam said in a breathy voice.

"That mantel is breathtaking when it's all decked out in flowers," Nancy said. "You don't have to decide right now. Take your time to think about it."

She moved them to the back of the house. "Restrooms are down that hallway. The bride and groom's rooms are upstairs. The only people allowed upstairs are the bridal party."

Nancy opened one of a trio of sliding glass doors, and they walked onto the screened-in porch. "As you can see, this area has plenty of room for a bride and groom table, round tables for your guests, and a wedding pie table. You'll have lots of space for the dance floor and disc jockey."

"This will all work perfectly," Carol said.

Pam nodded her agreement.

Nancy checked her watch. "I need to get back to my office for my next appointment. Feel free to wander the grounds if you'd like." She shook hands with both of them. "It's been a pleasure to meet you. You've got my card—reach out to me with questions. We've moved through things pretty fast this morning." She ushered them into the backyard from the covered porch with a "See you soon," and headed back the way they'd come in.

Carol turned to Pam. "Great choice. You're going to have a beautiful wedding. Did you want to roam around here? We have ten minutes before we need to leave."

Pam pointed to the stand of trees in front of them. "Would you like to see the meadow where Steve proposed? It's so pretty."

"You know I would!"

Pam headed down the path through the woods to the break in the fence, Carol close on her heels.

CHAPTER 15

"*T*his asparagus and gruyère quiche is delicious," Lori said, spearing her last bite with her fork.

"The crust is flaky and tender. Better than my own," Irene agreed. "The spinach and strawberry salad on the side is the perfect accompaniment."

"The Crooked Porch Cafe never disappoints," Carol said.

Irene dabbed her lips with her napkin. "I love hearing about your progress this morning. You're well on your way to having everything decided."

"The venue sounds lovely," Lori said. "I remember when it was a family home. It was gorgeous back then."

Carol looked at Pam, who had barely touched her lunch. "Aren't you hungry?"

Pam grinned sheepishly. "I guess I'm distracted, thinking about your dress."

"I understand completely. Deciding on your wedding dress is a big deal. Let's see if it works for you." Carol stood. "It's hanging on my closet door. I found a crochet hook this morning to fasten all those buttons down the back. We'll get you into it and you can see what you think."

"Will you come out to show us?" Irene asked.

"Of course."

"But the only opinion that counts is yours." Carol's tone was firm. "There's no pressure to like my dress. If you don't feel it's the one for you— even if all three of us love it—then you must say 'no' to the dress and we'll find the one of your dreams."

"Absolutely," Lori and Irene said in unison.

"Thank you," Pam smiled into the three sets of earnest eyes staring at her.

"We'll put your plate aside so you can eat after you've tried it on," Lori said. "You might be hungry then."

"Great idea," Carol said, picking up her empty plate.

"We'll clear the table." Irene took Carol's plate from her. "The two of you go get Pam into that dress. Lori and I are as excited as you are."

Irene and Lori busied themselves cleaning up after the takeout lunch.

Pam followed Carol up the stairs to the master bedroom. Carol stepped to one side when they entered the room and pointed to the wedding gown hanging on the back of the closet door, its train puddling on the floor.

Pam was drawn to the gown as if it possessed its own gravitational force. She sucked in a breath as she reached out a hand to touch the delicate fabric. Seed pearls outlined the sweetheart neckline. Lace panels, gathered at the waist, fanned in a wide arc across the full skirt. Sequins placed at random intervals caught the light, giving the dress a sense of motion when she touched it.

Carol stood to one side, biting her lip as she watched Pam's reaction. "If you don't like it, you don't have to try it—"

"Don't like it?" Pam cut her off. "It's the most beautiful dress I've ever seen. The photos don't do it justice."

Carol let out a breath in a whoosh. "I wasn't sure. You were so quiet."

"I'm in awe." Pam released the piece of the tulle skirt she was holding. "I can't believe you'd let me wear this."

"Don't be silly. I'd be thrilled for you to get

married in my dress." Carol removed the dress from the hanger and inserted her arms through the neckline to the waist. "I remember how they got me into this thing when I got married. It's no simple task."

Pam wriggled out of her T-shirt and jeans. She raised her arms over her head and bent toward Carol, who slipped the garment over Pam's head and pulled it down her body.

Pam straightened and Carol twisted and pulled at the massive dress until it was in place.

Carol snatched the crochet hook from the nightstand and meticulously secured the long row of covered buttons down the back of the dress. "The fit is perfect," Carol said. "You don't need any alterations."

Pam smoothed the fabric along her torso. "It feels great. And I have room to breathe."

"There's a full-length mirror on the other side of the closet door," Carol said. "Take a couple of steps back so I can close the door. I'll pick up the train."

Pam moved with Carol's help.

"Close your eyes," Carol said. "Let me arrange your train around you before I close the door. I'll tell you when you can open them to look in the mirror. I want you to get the total effect."

"Good idea." Pam closed her eyes.

Carol fussed with the dress, checking Pam's reflection in the mirror. "There. You can open them."

Pam inhaled sharply as she viewed her reflection, bringing her hands to her throat.

Carol chuckled. "That's what Cinderella did when she first saw herself in that blue ball gown."

Pam struggled to find her voice. "I *feel* like Cinderella."

"You like it?"

Pam nodded her head in agreement, then stopped and shook her head no. "I don't like it, I *love* it."

Carol reached out and squeezed Pam's shoulder. "I'm so happy to hear that. You look incredible."

"If I tried on a hundred dresses—*a thousand dresses*—I wouldn't find one I like better."

Carol stood behind Pam and put her hands on Pam's hips, looking over Pam's shoulder at their reflection. "I'm a bit shorter than you are. The dress is the perfect length on you now—in bare feet—but it may be too short when you're in heels."

"No worries there," Pam said. "I won't wear heels. This gives me the perfect reason to wear flats."

"Smart girl," Carol said. "I kicked mine off halfway through the reception. Those satin sandals rubbed my feet raw."

"My veil got lost by the dry cleaner," Carol said, "so we'll have to get that."

"I'll wear my hair down, around my shoulders," Pam said. "I'd like a simple, short veil."

"Lovely. Shall we show our mothers?"

Pam nodded. "We've been gone so long, I'm surprised they haven't come looking for us." She and Carol maneuvered the dress in a 180-degree turn and made their way down the stairs—slowly—and back to the dining room.

Pam paused in the arched entryway to the room, illuminated by sunlight from the bay window behind her. Pam's smile outshone the sequins.

Both mothers gasped.

"Oh, my ... " Lori uttered.

Irene blinked rapidly and fished in the pocket of her cardigan for a tissue.

"Did you ... say 'yes' ... to the dress?" Lori choked out.

Pam glanced at Carol, who winked at her.

"Yes. I most certainly did."

$\mathcal{N}$eva rose part of the way out of her chair and waved to Laura and her mother as they stood in the entrance to the tearoom at The Wishing Tree Inn. Afternoon tea was in full swing. The room hummed with conversation as servers moved through the space, refreshing pots of tea and refilling trays of tea sandwiches and scones.

Laura spotted Neva and the two women seated with her at a table by the front window. She tugged at the straps of her backpack as she and her mother made their way across the crowded room.

"I'm so glad you could come," Neva said, pointing to two empty chairs.

Laura slid into the one next to Neva.

"Would you mind terribly if I left Laura with you for half an hour? Arrangements fell through and I need to pick up my son from school and drop him off with his math tutor. I'll be back as soon as I can."

"That's fine," Neva said. "We'll save you some scones."

Laura's mother touched her daughter's shoulder. "Will you be all right without me?"

"Sure. I've got all my notes in here." Laura unzipped her backpack and removed a well-worn spiral notebook and a stack of pages printed from the Internet.

Her mother looked from Neva to Paige, and then to Irene. "Laura's been scouring the Internet ever since you called to invite her to join this group, Neva. She's full of ideas of ways to use the new shelter."

"That's exactly what we need," Paige said. "I've helped Laura pick out books at my bookstore." She smiled at the girl. "I know she's got a keen intellect and will have terrific suggestions."

"If it weren't for Laura, we wouldn't be getting this new shelter," Irene said. "She deserves to be part of this group more than anyone else."

Laura's mother flushed with pride at the kind words about her precocious daughter. "I'd better go. I'll be back soon."

"It looks like you've brought us some good ideas,"

Neva spoke to Laura. "Would you like to eat before you show us what you've brought to share?"

"Yes, please," Laura answered.

Paige held the tiered tray of sandwiches out to the girl. "Help yourself," she said. "There's egg salad, chicken salad, salmon with cream cheese, and cucumber."

Laura reached toward the tray, her hand hovering uncertainly.

"You can take one of each," Neva said. "And if you take a bite and you don't like it, you don't have to finish the sandwich."

Laura loaded her plate with one of each kind of sandwich.

"You'll want a scone, too. May I?" Irene asked.

Laura nodded, and Irene placed a scone next to Laura's sandwiches.

Neva poured tea for Paige and Irene as they filled their plates. "Tea, Laura? Or would you rather have a glass of milk?"

"Milk. Thank you."

Neva signaled a server and ordered Laura's beverage. Everyone nibbled on their food.

"As you know, we're here to advise Jed on other ways to use the shelter property. Duncan's will continue to own the shelter and the property, but it's clear that this project captivates the entire community. Jed asked me to gather a group together to advise him." Neva stirred honey into her tea and took a sip before continuing. "I believe the three of us," she gestured to Paige and Irene, "are wired into our community. Nothing happens in Linden Falls without one of us knowing about it."

Paige and Irene both chuckled. "There's some truth to that," Irene said.

"And Laura, here," Neva smiled at the girl, "is the heart and soul of this project. I suspected you'd bring all sorts of suggestions with you today. Would you like to tell us about what you found?"

Laura drained her glass of milk and swiped at her milk moustache with the back of her hand. "I've made a list," she said, pulling her spiral notebook off the empty chair next to her. "I searched online and found what other shelters are doing." She flipped to the first page. "I've got a lot of ideas. Mom said we can't do all of them. Some may cost too much money. She helped me put them in order." Laura looked up at the women leaning toward her.

Paige grinned, and Irene nodded in encouragement.

"First," Laura said. "We need a name for our shelter."

"That was on my list to discuss, too," Paige said.

"Have you got a suggestion?" Neva asked, even

though she had already read, upside down, the name Laura had printed in her notebook in glittery rainbow colors, decorated with stars.

"Fur Friends Sanctuary," Laura said in tones that conveyed glittery rainbow colors and stars. "I looked up words that would mean all animals would be safe there. That's why I picked sanctuary."

Irene turned to Paige. "That's a terrific name."

"I think so, too," Paige said.

"Mom said we should have a contest to name the shelter. She told me I could enter, but not to get my hopes up."

"I thought about a contest," Neva said. "But we don't need one. I love the name you suggested. It's Jed's decision, of course, but I'm in favor of recommending Fur Friends Sanctuary."

Paige and Irene nodded their agreement.

"I know my brother will love it," Paige said, "and now we've already got our name. That feels like significant progress."

"What other ideas have you got?" Irene asked.

Laura shared the results of her research, passing around the copies of webpages she'd printed out that supported her ideas.

The three women listened, asked questions, and reviewed the printouts.

"This is incredible," Irene said, stacking the

papers into a neat pile. "You are a force to be reckoned with, Laura."

Laura bit her lip and looked up uncertainly.

"That's a compliment, dear," Neva said, smiling at her.

"You've supplied enough ideas to come up with a five-year plan," Paige said. "I think we agree we should start with a dog park and a gift shop to benefit the shelter. I can offer dog- or cat-themed books—training guides, books about various breeds, or storybooks."

"I've been selling collars and bandanas at my booth at the farmers market, with all proceeds going to the shelter," Irene said. "They've been going like hotcakes. I'll put them in the gift shop, too. Other local craftspeoplc will also be interested."

"I'll bet someone will want to open a pet grooming service there. The dog park would be an excellent source of customers," Neva said.

"Jed's been talking to veterinarians from Linden Falls and three of the surrounding towns," Paige said. "They'd like to open an emergency vet clinic in part of the space."

"That would be wonderful. The closest one is over a hundred miles away," Irene commented.

"None of our towns are large enough to support one, but the shelter's location is between all four towns and the veterinarians think it will be successful."

"I love that idea," Neva said. She looked up to see Laura's mother hurrying across the tea room to join them.

"I'm sorry I'm late," her mother said, sinking into the empty chair next to Laura.

"Wait until you hear about all the progress we've made," Neva said. "Thanks to Laura." She filled a teacup and passed it to the frazzled woman. "Help yourself to sandwiches and scones while Laura fills you in."

The little girl sat up straighter in her chair and proudly announced the name of the shelter before relaying the rest of their decisions.

CHAPTER 17

*P*am plopped down on the edge of her bed and kicked off her black pumps. She lay back on the mattress and rubbed her sore feet together. It had been weeks since she'd worn anything other than athletic shoes or work boots.

Leopold crawled out from his lair under her bed and hopped up next to her. He melded his body to hers, meowing for attention.

Pam pulled him close and stroked his fur until he settled into the crook of her body. "You've been alone a lot, haven't you? I'm sorry about that. Between work and filming all day every weekend, I'm never home."

Leopold uttered a simple "Meep."

Pam turned onto her side and drew her legs onto the bed. She buried her face in her cat's neck. "Today was Ann Wilson's funeral. She was one of my clients. I loved her—everyone loved her." Her voice cracked. "You should have seen the crowd at her service."

Pam's phone vibrated in the pocket of her black shirtdress. She fished it out and answered when she saw the caller was Steve.

"Hi, sweetheart."

Pam sniffed. "Hi," she replied in a small voice.

"I'm just checking on you. A couple people came into the gym who were at Ann's service. They all said it was very moving."

"Her son gave a touching eulogy. The flowers were out of this world. Ann would have been so pleased."

"What do you plan to do the rest of the day?"

"I canceled all my clients and thought I'd take a nap." She glanced at the grid of sunlight outlining the shutters on her bedroom window. "But the sun's finally come out—after all these weeks of rain. Maybe I'll go for a walk instead."

"Would you like some company?"

"Don't you have clients this afternoon?"

"Nope. Everyone canceled. I think they all went to the funeral, too."

"You mean we could actually spend some time together, just the two of us?" She stood, picked up her pumps, and walked to her closet.

"That's what I have in mind. I miss you."

"I'd love that—with one modification."

"What would that be?"

"It needs to be the three of us. Bring Chance along."

Steve chuckled. "Good call. I'll grab him and pick you up in fifteen minutes. I know exactly where we should go."

"I'll be ready," Pam said. She swiped off the call, switched her phone off of silent mode, and shed her funeral clothes and somber mood.

"YOU'RE TAKING us to the field behind Enchanted Grove Estate, aren't you?" Pam pointed to a barn in the distance. "I recognize that."

Steve grinned. "Is that all right with you?"

"It sure is. Chance loved running off-leash through that field. He—and Leopold—have suffered a bit because of our busy schedules."

"I know. I feel guilty."

Pam swiveled in her seat to look at Chance, sitting upright on the back seat, his tongue hanging out as he panted in anticipation. "We're sorry you haven't had as many walks as you'd like, boy," she cooed in a sing-song voice. "We're almost done with this new animal shelter. It's sort of like the one where I found you—except animals can stay at the one we're building until they find their forever homes."

"I'm grateful that the workers at his shelter refused to follow protocol to put him down when he'd been there too long." Steve's voice wavered with emotion at the thought of how close his beloved dog had come to being euthanized. He slowed his SUV and pulled onto the dirt road leading to the field.

They parked, and the three of them tromped through the underbrush of trees lining the field. Chance pulled at his leash in anticipation.

"I think he remembers this place," Pam said.

"Maybe." Steve stooped and unhooked the leash. "Okay, boy!"

Chance leapt into the field. The grass had grown tall, coming up to his shoulder. Chance got a world-class case of the zoomies and was soon zigzagging from one end of the field to the other.

Pam and Steve tried to follow him, but the dense pack of vegetation impeded their progress.

"The recent heavy rains have caused growth to explode." Pam pointed to a large rock marooned at the edge of the field. "Let's sit up there to watch him."

Steve took her hand and helped her make her

way to the flat top of the rock, then scrambled up and sat next to her.

"I love how green everything is," Pam said.

"It's pretty." Steve sighed, looking at the verdant view. "For now."

"What do you mean by that?"

"I train several firefighters. They're worried about fire danger this fall if the weather pattern dries out."

"Is that likely?"

"Who knows? They tell me the weather patterns appear to predict average rainfall."

"Sounds like there's nothing to worry about," Pam said. She pulled her knees to her chest and hugged them to her. "Carol says Enchanted Grove Estate is more beautiful than ever, too."

Steve smiled at her. "Is that a hint? Do you want to slip through the fence again to look?"

Pam shook her head. "This grass is too long. I don't have the energy. Carol was there last week to go over final details with our coordinator, and she told me how stunning the grounds were. That's good enough for me."

Steve put his arm around her, and she rested her head against his shoulder. A trio of butterflies hovered around them, then flitted away.

"This is so peaceful and perfect. I don't want to move," she said.

"Almost perfect," Steve said, cupping her chin with his hand and pressing his lips to hers.

They were still kissing when Chance raced across the field toward them. Their idyllic interlude came to an abrupt end. A familiar odor preceded him.

Pam pulled away from Steve and they looked at each other in horror as recognition dawned on them.

"Skunk!" Steve cried.

Chance arrived at the rock and jumped up onto it.

Pam clamped her hand over her nose.

Steve hopped off the rock. "What have you done, you silly dog?" He extended a hand to Pam.

She took it and slid off the rock. "We'll have to roll the windows down and drive back to town."

"I'll drop you at your place and take him home to deal with this."

"I've got a better idea," Pam said. "We finished the dog washing stations at the new shelter. Let's take him there. It'll be far easier to bathe him in those special stations than in your bathtub."

"That's a genius idea. I have keys." He rubbed the back of his hand across his watering eyes. "You don't mind helping?"

"We're a team," she said. "You, me, Chance, and Leopold. Of course I'll help." She tapped at the screen of her phone. "This website says we'll need hydrogen peroxide, baking soda, and dish soap."

"We'll need to stop at the store," Steve said.

Chance lifted his muzzle and barked, his tail wagging. He sidled up to Steve, rubbing against his master's thigh.

"He has no idea how awful he is," Steve said, pushing the dog away from him.

Pam struggled not to gag. "No, he doesn't. Let's get out of here. The sooner we clean him up, the better."

CHAPTER 18

Steve and Pam stood in front of the entrance to Fur Friends Sanctuary and faced the camera.

The cameraman held up three fingers, then two, then one—and nodded. A close up of their faces appeared in the camera's frame.

"Welcome back to *Wishes of Home,*" Steve said. "Our work here at Fur Friends Sanctuary is almost complete and we're on track for our grand opening October 12. Pam and I will give you a sneak peek this week at what the community of Linden Falls has accomplished. We've got three special guests with us to help with our tour."

The camera pulled back to reveal a little girl with an unruly shock of blonde hair corralled by a pink ribbon, a small tan and white terrier, and Chance. The girl waved at the camera.

"Laura Thompson is with us today. She won last year's contest to suggest the project for this season of *Wishes of Home*. Laura has been involved with fundraising and planning for the project ever since. She's here with her dog, Rusty."

"Steve's dog, Chance, is our other guest." Pam patted the top of his head. "Both dogs are rescues. We thought you'd enjoy a dogs-eye-view of the facility."

"Cut," yelled the director. "That was super. We'll head into the dog park now. Just keep talking and we'll continue to film. Let the dogs run around, explore, and play. That's what viewers want to see."

They moved into the fenced area and released the dogs.

"You're sure Rusty can't get out?" Laura asked.

"I walked the entire length of fence yesterday," Pam assured her. "It's secure."

Chance and Rusty sniffed each other in greeting. When they'd finished their doggy hellos, they bounded from benches set beneath trees to a large grassy area in the center, and then to an area with three pieces of agility equipment.

"As you can see, we've got a double hoop jump, a

barrel, and a Corgi climb." Steve walked to the barrel and encouraged Chance to go through it.

The big dog balked, but Rusty zoomed through without hesitation and then doubled back to do it again.

Laura giggled and clapped her hands.

"This equipment is only the beginning. In time, we plan to raise enough money to purchase additional items," Steve said.

"You can also donate money to underwrite your— or your dog's—favorite piece of equipment," Pam said. She walked over to a shiny red fire hydrant. "Like this spray fire hydrant, donated by Linden Falls Fire Station Number 1." She called Chance and he ran to her. Pam pushed a button on top of the hydrant and a special valve dispensed a six-foot fan of mist.

Chance frolicked in the water, trying to catch it in his mouth.

The mist shut off automatically.

Chance gave himself a mighty shake and ran off in the opposite direction.

Pam, who had been standing near Chance, brushed water droplets from her clothing. Laura's peals of laughter brought Pam's attention back to the agility area.

"Rusty's good at this!" she shrieked. The little dog

jumped through the lower hoop, then turned, got a running start, and cleared the higher hoop. "He's never done this before." Rusty raced up one side of the Corgi climb and down the other.

"You've got a natural-born agility dog," Steve said, encouraging the pup to complete the course again. As they filmed, the lightning-fast Rusty completed the course with increasing speed each time. When the small dog finally plopped onto the grass, panting and exhausted, they turned their attention back to the rest of the park.

Chance was in a shady corner, behind the benches, wriggling on the ground.

"We'll now take you inside for a first look at the dog-washing station," Steve said into the camera. He whistled for Chance, who sprang to his feet and bounded across the park to where they stood.

The dog skidded to a stop and sat at their feet. His tail swept the ground and his hopeful eyes swung from Steve to Pam and back again.

Steve groaned. "Leave it to my dog to find—and roll in—the only mud puddle within reach."

"Look at you." Pam placed her hand under Chance's muzzle and turned it toward her. "We didn't tell you not to roll in the mud, so we can't be mad." She glanced at Steve. "I think this means we get to show our viewers how our new dog-washing stations work."

They exchanged a glance that said they were glad they'd had the opportunity to try them out earlier.

"Come on, Chance," Pam said, leading the way to the tiled room with three elevated porcelain sinks along one wall. Stacks of towels were stored under the sinks in cubbies. Shampoo in a large pump bottle stood at the ready. Hair dryers hung on the opposite wall.

Chance walked up the three stairs to one sink and stepped into place.

"He looks like he knows what he's doing," Laura said.

Pam and Steve smiled at each other. Pam grabbed the spray nozzle, turned on the water, adjusted the temperature, and began Chance's bath.

CHAPTER 19

"I'll help you with these," Pam said to her mother.

Irene placed the plastic tote onto the cart and turned away from the back of her SUV to look at her daughter. "What are you doing here?"

"I came to help with your booth at the farmers market."

"Aren't you filming today?"

Pam shook her head. "We're waiting on delivery of our order of crates for cats and small dogs. All the large dog runs have been completed. The reception area, visitation rooms, intake exam rooms—even the employee break room—are finished. We don't have anything to film until we get those crates. Marty canceled filming this weekend." Pam lifted the final two totes out of Irene's SUV and placed them on the cart.

Irene slung her purse over her shoulder and pressed her key fob to lock her SUV. "Will this delay the opening of the shelter?"

"No. Jed will buy them from another supplier, if necessary. The grand opening is still on schedule." Pam pulled the cart behind her.

"Thank goodness. We don't want anything to interfere with your wedding."

"Jed and Marty are aware of that. They've both RSVP'd that they're attending. Don't worry about anything messing up the wedding."

"That's a relief." Irene walked along with her daughter. "You didn't have to get up early to help at my booth. I've managed without you on Saturday mornings. Why don't you go home and crawl back into bed?"

Pam smiled at her mother and shook her head. "I woke up at 4:00 like I always do. Couldn't get back to sleep. It's fun working your booth at the market." She gestured to the town square, buzzing with energy and conversation as vendors exchanged cheerful banter while they set up their booths. "I missed this all summer while we were filming. Before you know it, the market will shut down for the winter. I couldn't wait to surprise you this morning."

They reached the spot where Irene had been selling her handmade table linens—and now dog collars and bandanas—for more than a decade. The two women set up the booth with practiced precision. Colorful displays of linens featuring the warm rusts, golds, and oranges of fall were neatly arrayed by the time the market opened at 8:00.

"The weather forecast is for a mild, sunny day," Irene said as the first customer approached. "We should be busy."

Busy they were. Pam was restocking the dog collar display from a plastic tote stored under a table when a smartly dressed woman close to her mother's age walked into the booth. A man followed along behind her. She soon had a tall stack of fall-themed placemats, napkins, and matching table runners set aside at the register.

"You remember that we have to take all that back to Westbury on an airplane, don't you, Maggie?"

Maggie Martin gave the man a side-eye. "Hmmm … Good point, John. We may have to buy an extra suitcase for our trip home. Since we're hosting Thanksgiving again this year, I'd like something new for our table, and these linens are gorgeous."

"I figured you'd come up with a solution." John Allen chuckled. "Buy whatever you want. We haven't had a real vacation since our honeymoon, years ago. You're overdue for some souvenir shopping."

Maggie shot him a smile and added another armload to her stack. "Look," she said, pointing to the display that Pam was restocking. "Let's get new collars for Roman and Eve."

"I'm *sure* they'll be disappointed if we don't bring them something," John quipped.

Maggie stepped to the display and began examining the options. "I'd love them to have matching collars."

John leaned over to examine the sign at the base of the display. "Buy all you want," he said. "The proceeds go to support a new no-kill animal shelter that will service this region. I can get behind that effort."

"I love the sound of that," Maggie said, selecting three sets of matching collars. She took them to her stack of linens and signaled to Irene that she was ready to check out.

John lingered at the dog collar display. He took out his wallet and handed one hundred dollars in twenties to Pam. "Put this toward the shelter."

"That's so nice of you! Are you from around here?"

He shook his head. "My wife and I are on vacation. We're leaf peepers."

"Wow. That's doubly nice."

"I'm a veterinarian. Your cause is close to my heart."

Pam stuck out her hand and introduced herself.

John shook it. "I'm John Allen. That's my wife, Maggie Martin, at the register. We're from Westbury."

"Consider yourselves honorary residents of Linden Falls," Pam said. "I hope you enjoy your visit, and come back again."

"I have a feeling Linden Falls is going to become very important to us," John said.

After a parting, "Thank you," Pam turned her attention to a customer with a question.

John joined Maggie in time to carry their purchases out of the booth.

CHAPTER 20

"*H*ey, good lookin'."

Steve's greeting at the other end of the phone line always made Pam smile. "What're you up to?"

"I'm about to take Chance for a walk. We spent our day off doing a much-needed deep clean of my place, followed by a big grocery shop. I picked up a couple of gorgeous steaks in the hopes that you'd join us."

"I'd love to." She yawned and stretched. "Leopold and I just woke up from a nap."

"Did you help your mom at the market this morning?"

"Yep. It was so busy. I met the nicest couple here on vacation. Can't wait to tell you about them."

"Do you want to go with Chance and me?"

"Sure. Can we take a ride past Enchanted Grove Estate? I'd planned to drive by this afternoon to see how the trees look since our wedding is in two weeks."

"You want to know if your vision of resplendent fall foliage is going to come true?"

"Kinda."

"A lot can change in two weeks," he said.

"I know. I still want to drive by."

"What do you think, boy? Are you up for a ride in the car?"

Chance woofed.

"See," Pam said. "He wants to go, too. We can stop at the field to let him run."

"And risk another skunk encounter?"

"That's not likely to happen again."

"We're on our way," Steve said.

Thirty minutes later, they rounded the curve in the road leading to the wedding venue. Steve slowed down.

Pam lowered her window and leaned out to look up at the treetops. "It's happening!" She pulled her head back in and pointed to the trees. "They're just starting to turn."

"Unless we have a cold snap or a rainy spell, the colors should be spectacular. Our wedding day may be at the peak of the season."

Pam checked her weather app. "It shows dry and hotter than normal temperatures for the next ten days." She clutched the phone to her chest. "It'll be perfect."

Steve pulled his SUV into a U-turn and they drove past the venue again before proceeding to the turnoff for the field.

Chance began barking the moment they pulled off the highway.

"You know this place, don't you, Chance?" Pam reached her arm through the center console opening and gave him a pat.

Chance gave her hand a slobbery kiss.

"We'll let him run off his zoomies," Steve said. "Then we need to get back. I want to start baked potatoes to go with our steaks."

"I'm in favor of that," Pam said.

They parked in their now familiar spot, and Chance was once more racing from one end of the field to the other.

Pam shielded her eyes from the sun and gazed at Enchanted Grove Estate from the back side. "You can see the trees even better from here." She pointed. "They're definitely turning."

Steve's gaze moved to the spot she was indicating. Then he took a step forward, his shoulders tense. A frown erased his smile like a cloud obliterating the sun.

"What?"

Steve gestured to the sky above the tree line. "Do you see that?"

Pam strained her eyes to see what he was looking at. "It's hazy. Sort of smokey. Like when someone has a bonfire in their backyard."

He nodded. "That's smoke, all right. And it's not from a backyard." He swung his arm in a wide arc. "It's all along our sight line."

Her eyes widened. "You don't think …?"

"I do. It's a wildfire."

"But we don't get those in Connecticut." She swallowed hard. "Do we?"

"Not the ones caused by lightning strikes. Our forest fires have been man-made."

They stood together, watching the sky.

"There's a lot of fuel for fires after our rainy spring and summer. And if the app I just looked at is right, we're heading into a hot, dry stretch of weather." She brought her hands to her temples. "I can't get the videos of those poor people fleeing from the fires in Paradise, California, out of my head. It was absolutely terrifying."

Steve reached for her. "That won't happen here.

If there is a fire, it's a long way off. Firefighters know how to handle this."

She turned to him and rested her head on his shoulder. "Call me crazy, but I think I smell smoke."

He inhaled deeply, then stepped back quickly and whistled for Chance. "Let's get to my house and turn on the news. We'll drive ourselves crazy with speculation."

Pam nodded her agreement.

The three of them piled into Steve's SUV and headed home.

CHAPTER 21

*J*ed took the stairs two at a time to the second-floor weight-training rooms at Linden Falls Fitness.

Steve was finishing up a session with a Wednesday afternoon client in the room at the top of the stairs.

Jed hurried to his side, out of breath from exertion.

"What's up?" Steve asked. He handed a set of dumbbells to his client. "This is our final set of curls." The man began to work with the weights.

"You know how the fire destroyed a shelter in the next town and all of their animals were moved into Friends for Life?" Jed bent over and rested his hands on his knees.

"I heard that on the news yesterday. Friends for Life had to double up some of them, but they took all the animals. None of them got hurt in the move."

Jed straightened. "The wind shifted this morning. The fire is now headed for Friends for Life."

Steve's client lowered the dumbbells to the floor. "It was really windy out when I got here half an hour ago. How close is the fire?"

Jed wiped his hand across his brow. "Close enough that they're evacuating Friends for Life. They called me to ask if they could bring the animals —all of them—to Fur Friends Sanctuary."

"You're not open until Saturday," the client said.

"What did you tell them?" Steve asked.

"I said yes. There's no other choice. We have to open the shelter—right now."

"Totally agree," Steve said. "It's the right thing to do."

"That's why I'm here," Jed said. "The crates we ordered just got delivered. We need help to assemble them, put them in place, and intake the animals from Friends for Life."

"I'll help," the client said.

"Thank you," Jed said to the man before addressing Steve. "I'm here to see if you and Pam could get away."

"Of course. We'll come as soon as we're done."

"There's no time to lose," Jed said.

"Cancel the rest of the day's sessions," Steve's client said. "I'm certain no one will mind."

"I'll get Pam and we'll head straight there."

"I hoped you'd say that. You can supervise the work. I'll continue spreading the word around town. I'm asking for volunteer workers and donations of dog and cat food, blankets, medical supplies—you name it."

"What about the staff you hired to start this weekend when we open?"

"Most of them are on their way."

Steve turned back to his client. "Sorry to cut you short. I'll give you a free session."

"You'll do no such thing. Round up Pam and I'll see you at the shelter."

PAM AND STEVE moved among the volunteers, answering questions and assisting with an extra pair of hands, as the crew assembled the hundred crates of various sizes.

Terry Grant, the general contractor, walked up to them as they were setting the final few crates in place. "I got here as soon as I heard," he said. "I was working a job almost a hundred miles away."

"No worries," Pam said, standing and stretching her back. "Everything's in place."

Steve's phone pinged, and he read the incoming message. He looked up at Terry and Pam. "That was Jed. They've begun transporting animals. The first group will arrive in twenty minutes."

"The intake staff is ready," Pam said. "Now that we've got a place to put the animals."

Steve hoisted himself onto a stainless-steel table and waved his hands over his head to garner attention. "That's it, everyone. We're ready—thanks to all of you who dropped everything and came to help. Friends for Life is evacuating, and the first group of animals will be here soon."

Someone began clapping, and the crowd took it up. Steve pulled Pam up next to him and they both joined in.

Steve's phone pinged again, and he read the message. "Jed says they've picked up strays along the way—animals that may have run away from their homes as the fire approached. He says most of them have singed fur and burned paws, but some are more seriously injured."

"What do you want us to do?" someone called out. "Should we stay to help?"

Steve turned to Pam.

"If you've got medical knowledge, yes. If not, go into town and spread the word that we need veterinarians and vet techs," Pam said.

"How about supplies—gauze, ointments, tape?" another volunteer asked.

"Good idea," Pam said. "If you can round them up and drop them off, that would be great."

The crowd dispersed as everyone set forth on their new mission.

As Jed had told them, the first group of evacuees consisted of a dozen anxiety-ridden cats and dogs from Friends for Life, plus another six dogs and one cat exhibiting various levels of trauma. Four of them barked nonstop while the others cowered in stunned silence.

"The two veterinarians in Linden Falls are swamped with walk-ins from people fleeing the burn areas with their injured pets," one of the intake staff told Pam. "One of them has sent a senior vet tech, but that's all the help we're going to get until their practices close for the day."

They both looked at a German shepherd whimpering pitifully as he pawed at his badly burned ears.

"We'll have to do the best we can," the staff member said.

Pam's eyes pooled with tears as she looked at the

array of miserable animals in front of her. "This is just the first wave," she said. "I don't know how to help them."

"No worries." A confident voice sounded behind her.

Pam turned to see the man from the farmers market, the generous donor in town on vacation —*the veterinarian*—walk up to her and the staff member. His wife, the pretty woman who had bought stacks of fall table linens from Pam's mother, was with him.

"I graduated veterinary school with one of your local vets," John said. "We're visiting him and his wife. Anyway—he just called to ask me to jump in here until he can get away."

Pam almost collapsed against him in relief.

Maggie put a reassuring arm around Pam's shoulders. "You're in great hands with John."

"Are you a veterinarian, too?"

"No. I came along to lend a hand." Maggie looked toward the kennel area. Dogs barked and howled, and cats meowed in distress. "I can at least provide comfort to these poor creatures."

"We picked up supplies on our way here." John assessed the scene in front of him. "We may need more."

"Extra supplies are on their way," the staff member said.

"Good to hear. Linden Falls knows how to hang together in a crisis." He approached the German shepherd. "We'll start with this fellow. Can you assist me?" he asked the staff member.

She hurried to his side and, together, they cleaned wounds, bandaged paws, and administered painkillers. Another van pulled up with more evacuees. Pam moved in to help unload them. Maggie joined her. The noise level in the shelter rose by a decibel. Maggie and Pam filled water bowls, distributed kibble, and calmly petted the distressed creatures, always speaking in comforting tones.

It was well after midnight when the last group of evacuees had been situated.

John and his veterinarian friend, who had arrived shortly before nine, finished their ministrations to the injured. They scrawled their cell phone numbers prominently on a whiteboard in case of additional emergencies.

Pam walked John and Maggie to their rental car. "I don't know what we would have done without you," she said, her voice cracking. "Linden Falls owes you one."

Maggie pulled the young woman into a tight hug.

They leaned together, propping each other up. "It's been quite a night," Maggie said.

"Not exactly the way you'd want to spend your vacation," Pam commented, releasing Maggie.

"On the contrary," Maggie replied. "I felt more needed—more useful—than I have in years." She glanced at her husband. "I can assure you that John was in his element. Nothing lights him up like helping a suffering animal."

Pam brushed her hair off of her face. "I hope you come visit us next year. Linden Falls will roll out the red carpet for you."

John looked at Maggie, then back at Pam. "We've had a wonderful time in your town. I think you can count on our return."

Pam watched as John and Maggie pulled out of the parking lot, then went back inside. Steve and Jed were huddled in the calm of the entryway that had been a sea of chaos only an hour earlier. An occasional bark broke the uneasy silence.

"I've never been through anything like this," Pam said.

"That was really something, seeing how everyone came together to help these guys. Even our visitors —John and Maggie," Steve said. "I'm three parts exhausted, and one part wired with adrenaline."

Jed laughed. "That's a good way to put it. I think

the two of you should head home while you still have that one part going for you."

"You're right. Let's go." Steve put his hand on the small of Pam's back and they moved toward the door.

"Aren't you coming, Jed?" Pam asked as he stayed put.

"There's a cot in the back. I'll sleep here."

"The night-shift staff is here. The animals won't be alone," Steve replied.

"I know, but this is the first night for our shelter and it's been traumatic. I'd be too worried to sleep if I went home, so I may as well stay."

Pam crossed to him and planted a kiss on his cheek. "You're a good man, Jed Duncan."

"Go on," he said, flushing at the unexpected compliment. "Chance is probably hungry and worried sick about you."

"I called my sister on the way here," Steve said. "Carol was going to feed him and let him out."

"Glad to hear it."

"We'll check on you in the morning," Pam said. "If you need anything in the meantime, call either of us."

Pam and Steve stepped out into the chilly night. The sky to the west glowed orange, and the smell of acrid smoke filled the air.

"It seems farther away to me," Steve said.

"Me too," Pam agreed.

"At least it's not moving toward us."

Pam's breath caught in her throat. She stopped abruptly and tugged on his elbow, her eyes expanding like pancake batter on a griddle. "I just realized—Enchanted Grove Estate is close to Friends for Life."

CHAPTER 22

Steve took Pam in his arms. "We don't know what's happened to Enchanted Grove Estate. I'm sure we'll find out tomorrow. Try not to worry about it tonight."

Pam took a deep breath. "You're right." She cupped his cheek with one hand. "If it's gone—if we can't have the wedding we've planned—I still want to marry you a week from Saturday."

He pressed a kiss into her palm. "I'm glad to hear you say that. Me too."

His cell phone rang in his pocket and caller ID informed him it was his home security company.

"You've got to take that," Pam said, releasing him.

Steve answered the call as they walked to his SUV. His pace increased as he listened. "There's an alarm at my house," he said as he unlocked the doors and flung himself behind the wheel.

"Fire?" Pam's voice telegraphed her alarm as she got into the passenger seat.

"Burglar," Steve said. "The police are on their way. I'll drop you at your house and meet them there."

"I'm coming with you," Pam said. "Don't waste time taking me home."

Steve didn't argue with her. Two police cars, lights flashing, sat in his driveway when they pulled up.

Steve parked at the curb and was out of his SUV in a flash. He bounded across the lawn to where two uniformed officers huddled together on the walkway to his front door.

Pam followed on Steve's heels.

One officer called Steve by name.

Steve nodded.

"Someone jimmied open your back door," he said. "That must have triggered your alarm and scared them away. We checked inside and it doesn't look like anything's missing. Televisions are still on the wall; money left out on top of the bedroom dresser is still there."

"What about my dog?" Steve asked.

"We didn't see any dog."

"Big, black Lab. Friendliest dog on the planet."

Both officers looked at him and shook their heads.

"No sign of him," the other officer said. "The back door was halfway open. He must have gotten out."

"Dogs get freaked out by this sort of situation," the first officer said. "He's probably hiding out close by. When he sees you, he'll come home. Would you mind looking inside to see if anything's missing?"

"If the TVs and money are there, I'm sure it's all fine. I want to look for my dog."

The officer nodded. "Call us if you later find that something's gone."

Pam, who had been listening to the conversation, stepped forward. "Is it possible Carol took him home with her?"

"I don't think so. She would have texted me if she had." He checked his phone. "Nothing from her."

"Let's start looking," Pam said. "I'll go up and down the street, calling for him."

"You're exhausted. I should take you home."

"I am *not* sleeping while Chance is out there ..." her voice cracked before she finished her sentence.

"Okay. I'll head to the back yard and work my way along the property lines. There's more foliage for him to hide in there."

The police cars shut off their flashing lights and

pulled away from the house. The night sky was illuminated by a distant orange glow. The only sound was the repeated shout of one word: *Chance*.

Pam and Steve continued their search, covering an area and then doubling back, shouting and listening for even the smallest sound to indicate the dog's presence. Their throats were dry and irritated from the smoke-polluted air.

Pam crossed the residential street and began a third pass when Steve caught up with her. "It's no use," he said, shaking his head. "Chance isn't here."

Pam stopped and turned sad eyes to his sadder ones.

"If he could hear us, he'd come out," Steve said.

She nodded. "I agree. He must have been terrified and ran off."

"Or maybe the burglars took him." Steve's tone was tinged with misery. "You know how friendly he is."

Pam considered this. "I don't think so. He's super protective of you. He'd understand that friends don't break into houses."

"You think so?"

Pam put her hands on his shoulders. "I do. We'll make signs and post them all over town tomorrow. Mom and Neva and Paige will all help. We'll post it on the community bulletin board in Millie King's supply store. And Duncan's. We'll find him. You'll see."

She hugged him tight. "We're both exhausted. Let's get some sleep and be back at it as soon as it's light out."

He nodded his agreement, and they trudged wearily toward his house.

CHAPTER 23

*P*am drove slowly along the town square and parked across from the famous Wishing Tree. She picked up the piece of cardstock she'd cut in the shape of a dog's paw. On it she'd written her simple wish: Bring Chance Home. She'd punched a hole at the top and threaded it with a thin length of red ribbon. The only thing she needed to do was hang it on the tree.

Pam crossed the street and walked to the tree. Dozens of wishes twirled in the light breeze. She stopped to read a few. All were like hers: people wanted the safe return of a pet who had run away during the fire.

Pam sent up a silent prayer for each one, then hung her wish for Chance on the tree. She returned to her car with one errand remaining on her list.

In the few days since Chance had gone missing, flyers with his photo and Steve's phone number had been placed at every register, taped in every shop window, and stapled to every tree around the square. Hearing about the call Steve had received early that morning had propelled her out of the gym during the free hour she had between clients.

Someone had seen a large black dog—maybe a Lab—skulking in the underbrush along the highway near Enchanted Grove Estate. They'd pulled onto the shoulder of the road and tried to coax the animal to come to them, but, in the end, it had run off in the opposite direction.

Maybe it was Chance, heading to the field he loved so much. Steve had planned to check out the lead as soon as he had finished up for the day, but she had to see for herself—right now.

Pam drove slowly along the road running behind the estate, keeping her eyes peeled for any motion on either side. She repeated the route three times, then pulled off onto the dirt road that led to the field.

She stapled one of the lost dog flyers to a large tree facing the highway, then walked the short distance to the place where they always entered the field. The grass in the field stood tall and untouched. If she glanced to her right, she saw a swath of trees in vibrant fall tones worthy of a picture postcard. To her left rose the charred spires of leafless trees that the fire had ravaged. The stone chimney of the gracious old home stood alone, the top outlined by a cloudless blue sky.

Pam brought her hands to her heart and clutched the front of her shirt. The fire had destroyed the lovely structure at the heart of the estate, but had stopped where the field intersected the property line of the venue. The field was still pristine.

She swiped at a tear that traced down her cheek and chastised herself for being sad about the change in her wedding plans. At Tom's urging, Carol had worked tirelessly to move the wedding and reception to her own home. Flowers, caterers, disc jockey, photographer—all had been amenable to the change of location. She'd rented tables and chairs, arranged for house cleaners, and scheduled tree trimmers and landscapers to manicure her yard.

Pam was marrying the man of her dreams and her sister-in-law-to-be was moving heaven and earth to make everything lovely for them. She was truly grateful. Now if they could just find Chance. The thought of the sweet dog—alone, undoubtedly hungry, and possibly hurt—brought a fresh round of tears.

She walked to the center of the field and turned

her back on the ravaged estate property. Even if the beautiful fall vista in front of her wouldn't be part of her wedding, she would enjoy the view now—and visualize Chance coming home.

She studied the glorious trees on the other side of the highway and didn't notice the woman at the wheel of the SUV slow down and take note of her before speeding away.

CHAPTER 24

*L*aura and her older brother jumped out of the car as soon as they parked in the Fur Friends Sanctuary and raced ahead of their mother to the door. Laura pulled on the handle and rapped on the glass when she found it locked.

A staff member passing through the lobby pointed to the sign posted on the door that the shelter would open to the public in four days.

"Mr. Duncan said we could look for our dog early." She raised her voice to be heard through the glass.

"Are you Laura Thompson?" the woman asked.

Laura nodded. "This is my brother."

Their mother walked up and the woman opened the door to let them in. "Jed told me to be on the lookout for you." She spoke to Laura. "Thank you for everything you did to make this shelter a reality. I think it's only right for you to be the first one to adopt a pet. Follow me." She turned and took them to the hallway leading to the kennels. "Large dogs are in the row on your right, and small breeds are to your left. Let me know if you'd like to take any of them to the get-acquainted area. We recommend it —adopting a dog is a huge commitment."

"Thank you," their mother said. "We'll do that." She looked at her children. "Where do you want to start?"

Laura and her brother turned to each other. "Large," they said in unison.

"Rusty is a small terrier mix," their mother cautioned. "He might be better with someone his own size."

Her children looked at her. "We want a big dog, Mom," her son said.

Laura's head pumped up and down like a piston. "We'll get a friendly dog," she said. "Like Chance."

Their mother sighed in resignation.

Laura and her brother traversed the rows of kennels twice, reading the posted signs about each dog. They studied all the occupants, talking to the dogs and sticking their fingers through the grates to scratch noses and accept licks.

At the end of their second pass, Laura's brother

turned to her. "I know which one I want. I think he's your favorite, too."

Laura pointed to the second kennel on the right. A dog sat calmly at the front of the kennel, his mouth open and tongue hanging out in a way that gave him a jaunty expression. His wavy brown coat resembled a teddy bear. "He's so cute. That's the one I want."

"Me too," her brother said. "The sign says he's a poodle and a golden retriever mix."

They returned to his kennel.

"It says Friends for Life picked him up as a stray —with no tags and he's not microchipped. They think he's two," her brother said.

Their mother joined them.

The dog brought his right paw up and stuck it through the wire grid, as if to shake hands.

Their mother chuckled and took the offered paw in her hands.

"You like him, too, don't you, Mom?" Laura asked, hope in her voice.

"I do," her mother said. "Let's take him to the get-acquainted area to spend time with him. We have to be sure about this."

"Dad's really gonna like him," Laura said.

Her mother signaled to the staff member that

they were ready for her help. The woman put the dog on a leash and they trailed after her.

"We'll have to name him," her mother said.

Laura slanted her eyes at her brother. "How about Bear? Since he looks like one?"

"I like it!" he replied. He raced ahead to catch up with the staff member. "Hey, Bear," he said, leaning over to stroke the dog's head. "What do you think of your new name?"

The dog swiveled his head to look back at the little girl, then glanced up at her brother, before emitting a single "Woof."

CHAPTER 25

Marty positioned Pam and Steve behind the yellow ribbon stretching across the double glass doors with the name Fur Friends Sanctuary painted on the glass in tall black script. Drawings of dogs or cats decorated the name by peeking out from behind the letters *F, F, S,* and y.

Jed stood in back of the huge yellow bow tied in the middle of the ribbon. Laura was at his side. For this occasion, her hair was restrained by a yellow ribbon. Bear sat at her feet, wearing a yellow bandana.

Marty handed him an oversized pair of scissors.

"I'll read my remarks, thanking the community for donating their time, talent, and treasure to make the shelter a reality. I'll introduce Laura—and Bear, our first adoptee." He grinned at the girl and dog who were already an inseparable pair. "Laura will announce the name of the shelter. Then Laura and I will cut the ribbon together and declare it officially open."

"Yep," Marty said. "Steve will step in and thank Duncan's Hardware for donating the land, building, and improvements."

"I'll talk about the evacuees from Friends for Life and announce that we're waiving adoption fees this week since we're already at capacity—because of the fire," Steve said.

Laura hopped from one foot to the other.

"You're bursting with excitement." Marty smiled at the girl.

"My family's adopting a cat—*today*," she said. "After we're done, Mom and Dad and my brother and me are going to pick her out. I want a girl." The pride in her voice was palpable. "Dad says I'm very responsible so we can get a cat."

"I'm so happy to hear this, Laura." Pam put her arm around her young friend and hugged her. "You'll give two deserving strays a very happy home. Rescues make remarkable pets." Pam looked at Steve, her eyes swimming with tears that were about to spill over.

He rubbed the moisture away from his own eyes and nodded at her.

"Marty, do you mind if I end by letting our viewers know about Chance?" Pam's voice shook and she took a steadying breath. "They know him from the earlier episode when we showed the dog park and dog washing stations." She held up a flyer. "I'd like to show this."

"Of course you can." He glanced at Steve. "That's got your phone number on it. Are you sure you want it out there?"

"If it leads to getting him back, I'm fine with it."

"Okay, everybody. Quiet on the set. We're ready to roll."

As planned, Pam made a heartfelt plea at the conclusion, begging anyone who might have seen Chance to contact Steve. Marty announced that season two of *Wishes of Home* was a wrap.

Jed told them all that he'd reserved the rear patio of Woody's Pizza for pizza, wings, beer, and soda for the cast and crew. His treat.

Cheers and a smattering of applause rose from the crowd. Laura joined her family and they headed for the cat crates as others went to their cars.

"You'll be there, won't you?" Jed asked Pam and Steve.

They looked at each other, and Steve shook his head. "The wedding is next Saturday, and we're spending tomorrow with my sister, going over the revamped plans for the ceremony and reception. Tonight is our only chance to relax."

Jed looked from one set of tired eyes to the other. "I understand. You've both worked so hard this past week. And now Chance." His voice cracked with emotion. "I know how I'd feel if Gladys or Bailey got lost."

Pam hugged him. "Thanks for not being mad."

Jed walked them to the door and opened it. "Go get some rest. We can't have the bride or groom showing up with bags under their eyes." Jed shook Steve's hand. "See you at Carol's next Saturday for the wedding."

CHAPTER 26

*P*am heard a light knock on her front door. Leopold stared at her from his perch on the kitchen counter, waiting for his breakfast. She quickly scooped kibble into his bowl and placed it on the floor. He leapt down and began eating.

She went to the door and peered through the peephole.

"Steve. What're you doing here?

"I'm picking up your overnight bags," he said.

"They're behind the chair to the right of the door. Where I told you they'd be."

"Well … okay … I see them." He leaned close to the door. "Can you open the door?"

"On our wedding day? Of course not. It's bad luck for the groom to see the bride."

"I thought that was just when you were in your wedding dress."

"Nope. I'm a traditionalist. That prohibition applies all day, until the ceremony."

"I've got a pumpkin spice latte for you." He held up a paper cup. "Your favorite. Made with oat milk. The foam on top is shaped like a heart."

She was silent.

"The bride—my bride—deserves to start her wedding day with her favorite drink."

He heard Pam chuckle.

"Put it down and turn around. I'm going to open that door and get my coffee. You *must not* see me."

He honored her wishes. "If I stay turned away from you, can you leave the door open to talk?"

The door creaked open.

Pam picked up the cup, removed the lid, and took a sip. "This is soooo nice of you. Thank you."

"My pleasure. What are you doing today—before the wedding?"

"My mom, your mom, Carol, and Emma are coming over in thirty minutes. The stylist from *Wishes of Home* is doing hair and makeup on each of us. I'm last, so it stays fresh for pictures."

"That's practically an all-day affair. It'll only take half an hour for your brother and me to shower, shave, and get dressed."

"Lucky you," Pam said. "It may take that long for my mom to button the back of my dress. Since you'll have so much free time, what are you and Kurt going to do? No … don't tell me. Let me guess—you're playing golf?"

Steve kept his back turned to her. "Nope. We thought about it but decided not to."

"You're going out to look for Chance again, aren't you?"

Steve nodded. "I can't shake the feeling that he's out there, trying to get home."

Pam swallowed the lump in her throat. "That's why you need to take my bags to your house. I don't want to spend the night at a romantic inn. We need to be there if—when—he comes home."

"Oh, babe. It's our honeymoon. We've only planned one night, for now. We shouldn't cancel it."

"That romantic inn will always be there. We're staying at your place until he comes home or …" Her voice cracked.

He shifted his weight to turn toward her.

"No!"

He resumed his stance with his back to her.

"Thank you," he said quietly.

"We've got plenty of time to settle in together here at my house, as planned. We'll know when the time is right to move out of yours."

A car pulled into the driveway.

"That's the stylist. Everyone else will arrive any minute. You'd better get out of here."

Steve picked up her bags and took one step off the porch. "You're the one and only one for me, Pam. I can't wait to marry you."

PAM'S HOUSE was a blur of activity as showers ran, hairdryers hummed, and conversation flowed, accentuated by frequent bursts of laughter.

The stylist braided Emma's thick hair into two long plaits wound with flowers and pinned to the top of her head.

"Look!" she cried when the stylist handed her a mirror so she could see the updo from every angle. "I look like a princess."

The women gathered around her.

"You're exactly like a princess," Pam said, smiling at her.

Carol, Irene, and Lori grinned at Emma. "You're pretty as a picture," her grandmother said.

By noon, Pam was the only person remaining to be styled. She hopped in the shower as Irene walked Carol, Emma, and Lori to the door.

"You've got a crochet hook for those buttons?" Carol asked.

Irene glanced at the magnificent gown laid out across Pam's sofa. "Yep. I brought two of them, just in case. If I have any trouble, I'll text you to come out to the car when we arrive at your house so you can fasten them."

"About that …" Carol cast a furtive glance at the closed bathroom door. "There's been a slight change of plan."

Irene's eyebrows shot up. "Again? I thought the wedding venue burning down right before the wedding would be enough."

Carol leaned in and whispered in Irene's ear.

A smile slowly spread from ear to ear as Irene listened. "That sounds absolutely perfect! If I wasn't worried about ruining both of our hair and makeup, I'd give you the tightest hug."

Carol grinned back. "I'm glad you approve. I wasn't sure I was doing the right thing."

Irene grabbed Carol's hand and squeezed it. "You are. We'll see you there at 3:55."

CHAPTER 27

*I*rene worked the crochet hook through the final loop of braided thread and secured the button. "There," she said, smoothing the gown over Pam's hips. She stood behind her daughter and looked at their reflections in the mirror.

Irene's bottom lids filled with tears, and she turned away, blinking rapidly. "You're resplendent, my dear." She snatched a tissue from the nightstand and dabbed at her eyes. "We need to get going. I don't have time to redo my makeup if I cry."

"Carol's house is less than ten minutes. We won't be late," Pam said. She turned, took the tissue from her mother, and smoothed away a smudge under her mother's right eye.

Irene stopped herself from blurting out that they weren't going to Carol's. "I'd still like to leave."

"If you're on time, you're late; and if you're early, you're on time. That's your motto." Pam gathered her voluminous skirt with both hands. "Goodbye, Leopold," she called toward the foot of her bed, where she suspected he was hiding. "Grandma will come by in the morning to feed you."

Irene helped Pam navigate the steps off the front porch and arranged the dress around her daughter in the passenger seat of her SUV.

"You look gorgeous in that purple dress, Mom. The color suits you," Pam said.

Irene flushed with pleasure. "I never wear this shade, but I like it."

"Now I know what to get you for Christmas," Pam said. "Maybe a purple sweater? Or a coat?"

They chatted amiably until they crossed through the town square and Irene put on her turn signal.

"Carol's is the other way, Mom." Pam furrowed her brows. "You know that."

Irene patted her daughter's knee. "I'm going the right way."

"What?"

"You'll see soon enough."

They pulled off the highway at 3:53. A dozen cars lined the dirt track running alongside the field.

Pam leaned forward, peering out the windshield.

A wide swath of the tall grass in the center of the field had been freshly mowed. White folding chairs were arranged in two sections, flanking a carpet runner that ran from the familiar entrance of the field to a trellised arch at the far end of the chairs.

Flowers in shades of peach, orange, cream, and mauve adorned the arch. Every chair had ribbons tied to them in the same tones. The late afternoon sun transformed the hills beyond the arch into a fiery display of fall foliage.

"Carol arranged all of this at the last minute because she thought you'd both love it."

Pam sucked in a breath and fanned her face with her hand. "So much! Now it's my turn to stop crying so I don't ruin my makeup." She shook her head in disbelief. "It's everything I wanted."

"The reception is still at Carol and Tom's," Irene said. "Now, I think I see your brother … and a groom waiting for his bride."

Pam nodded. "Plus a little girl who's bursting at the seams to be a flower girl."

Irene helped Pam get out of the car.

Carol met them at the beginning of the carpet runner. "You look beautiful in this dress," she whispered. She pulled the simple veil over Pam's face and handed Pam a bouquet of flowers that matched the arch. She worked with Irene to position Pam's train.

Irene reached under the veil to tuck a long curl of Pam's chestnut hair behind her shoulder. "This is one of the happiest days of my life," Irene said.

"It's *the* happiest day of mine, and I wish Dad was here to share it with us," Pam whispered.

"He is, honey." Irene glanced skyward. "I've felt his presence all day."

"Ready?" Carol asked.

Pam and Irene nodded.

Carol waved her arm above her head and the strains of *Pachelbel's Canon in D* filled the air. She tapped her daughter on the shoulder, and Emma started down the aisle, scattering ivory and peach rose petals. Carol followed her.

Pam tucked her hand into her mother's elbow. Steve's beaming smile as he sought her out beyond his niece and sister filled her heart until she thought it would burst. The sun broke through the high clouds, illuminating Pam in a wash of warm light.

Irene took a step forward and walked the bride to her groom.

Pam passed by her family and friends, unable to take her eyes off the love of her life, as if the two of them were the only ones present.

Steve leaned down and put his mouth to her ear. "You look stunning," he whispered.

Pam tilted her chin to him, and the look they shared held the energy of two magnets drawn irresistibly together.

The pastor cleared his throat, and the couple faced him. His short homily with readings from the Bible, Maya Angelou, and Shakespeare was followed by traditional vows.

Steve's rich baritone reached the tree line when he said, "I do." He repeated after the pastor the time-honored words as he placed the ring on Pam's finger.

Pam's clear voice resonated with conviction as she voiced her "I do," then raced ahead of the pastor as she recited her pledge from memory while placing Steve's ring on his finger.

Irene, Lori, and Carol all dabbed at their eyes with hankies from the front row.

"You may kiss your bride," the pastor said.

Steve gingerly lifted the short blusher veil over Pam's head and encircled her with his arms. Pam slid her hands up his back as she pressed herself against him. The couple melted into each other and kissed in a fashion that testified to their joy. They finally pulled apart.

The pastor was about to present the newly

married couple to the wedding guests when a disturbance at the edge of the field drew his attention.

A large black dog, its fur matted with dirt and full of twigs, barked once, and then again.

Pam dropped her bouquet and brought both hands to her throat.

Steve cupped his hands around his mouth. "Chance!" he shouted.

Everyone turned to look.

Chance dug in and bounded toward them, his paws barely touching the carpet runner as he flew across the distance that separated him from his family.

Pam dropped to one knee and held out her arms to the dog.

Steve stepped in front of her and scooped up the ecstatic dog, holding him while he wrestled and squirmed.

Chance sent his tongue out to lick anything it came into contact with.

When Chance had calmed down, Steve set him on the ground in front of Pam.

"No jumping," he admonished. "We don't want to mess up Pam's dress."

Chance wagged his tail ferociously but obeyed Steve's command.

Pam took his muzzle in her hands and kissed the

top of Chance's head. "I knew you'd find us," she whispered to him. "I *knew* it would be here."

Chance emitted one confirming bark, then turned.

The wedding march began to play, and Chance led them down the aisle.

THE END

EPILOGUE

Millie King felt the cold, moist nose of her faithful Golden Retriever tap her hand as a reminder that it was time to close the shop for the day. She looked at the clock and smiled down at Bingo, who was now squirming impatiently by her knees. If there was one thing Bingo knew without question, it was when it was time for her dinner. The dog's internal clock was as accurate as Greenwich Mean Time.

Millie finished tabulating the days' receipts and noted the figure on a spreadsheet. The Linden Falls post office branch's revenues were steady and the office and art supplies she also sold gave her a nice profit. She was happy that she'd moved to Linden Falls and opened the store.

Bingo uttered a short "woof" to remind Millie that she was still there.

"Ok, girl—I'm on it." Millie rose from the high stool behind the register and crossed to the door, Bingo trotting at her heels. Millie was turning the OPEN sign to CLOSED when she noticed the young woman jogging across the town square toward her shop, her ponytail swinging from side to side as it grazed her shoulders.

"Sit and stay," Millie commanded Bingo before opening the door to wave at Pam Olson.

Pam rushed across the street and paused in the doorway, panting. "I know I'm late," Pam said. "I've been trying to get here before closing ever since you called about that package. If you want me to come back another day, I'll understand. I don't want to put you out."

"Don't be silly, dear," Millie said. "The only one who's in a hurry is Bingo." She glanced at the dog who was looking from one to the other of them with pleading eyes. "She can wait ten minutes for her dinner."

"Thank you," Pam said, following Millie into the shop. "Steve and I are both more than curious to see what's in this package. We barely know Maggie Martin and John Allen."

"Based on my conversation with Maggie about the two of you—and the fact that she was excited to send you a wedding present but didn't have an address for you—I'd say you made a big impression on them." Millie retrieved a shoebox-sized parcel, wrapped neatly in brown paper. The sender had addressed the parcel to Pam Olson and Steve Turner in care of Millie King at the shop's address. "Not many people would attempt to have a parcel sent to a local post office branch and rely on the postmaster to get the parcel to its recipient." She put the box in Pam's outstretched hand.

"Gosh, it's heavier than I expected." Pam brought her other hand up to grasp the package. "They were the nicest older couple. She and I worked so hard together, settling in the animals relocated to the new shelter during the forest fire. I'm sure we would have lost some of the injured animals if John hadn't been there treating them. We were unbelievably lucky that a leaf-peeping veterinarian and his wife were visiting Linden Falls when the fire happened."

Bingo sneezed noisily, reminding them she was there.

"I'd better let you go," Pam said. "Thank you for staying open for me."

"No problem," Millie said. "To tell you the truth, I'm curious to know what she sent. Maggie told me it's an item from her home in Westbury. The house has a name: Rosemont. I was curious, so I looked it up online."

Pam arched an eyebrow.

"It's an absolutely gorgeous stone manor home. Like an English country house."

"Now I really can't wait to see what's in here." Pam gestured with the box. "We'll open it as soon as Steve gets home. I'll stop in on Saturday to show you, if you'd like."

"I'd love that," Millie said. "That's very nice of you."

"It's the least I can do." She bent to Bingo and gave her an ear rub. "Sorry to delay your dinner, girl." She opened the door and stepped outside. "See you soon."

Millie turned the sign to CLOSED and turned her full attention to Bingo.

❧

Don't miss any books in the Wishing Tree series:

★ Don't miss a Wishing Tree book! ★
Book 1: The Wishing Tree – prologue book
Book 2: I Wish.. by Amanda Prowse
Book 3: Wish You Were Here by Kay Bratt
Book 4: Wish Again by Tammy L. Grace
Book 5: Workout Wishes & Valentine Kisses by Barbara Hinske
Book 6: A Parade of Wishes by Camille Di Maio
Book 7: Careful What You Wish by Ashley Farley
Book 8: Gone Wishing by Jessie Newton
Book 9: Wishful Thinking by Kay Bratt
Book 10: Overdue Wishes by Tammy L. Grace

Book 11: A Whole Heap of Wishes by Amanda Prowse
Book 12: Wishes of Home by Barbara Hinske
Book 13: Wishful Witness by Tonya Kappes
Book 14: A Wish for Forgiveness by Amanda Prowse
Book 15: Wishful Tails by Barbara Hinske
Book 16: One More Wish by Tammy L. Grace
Book 17: A Wish in the Wind by Kay Bratt

WE ALSO INVITE you to join us in our My Book Friends group on Facebook. It's a great place to chat about all things bookish and learn more about our founding authors.

FROM THE AUTHOR

Thank you for reading the fifteenth book in THE WISHING TREE SERIES. I had such fun creating this world with my author friends from My Book Friends, and I hope you'll read all the books in the series. They're wonderful stories centered around a special tree in Linden Falls. If you enjoyed this story, I also hope you'll explore more of my work. You can find all my books on Amazon.

If you enjoy women's fiction, you'll want to try my bestselling ROSEMONT SERIES, filled with stories of friendship, family, romance, stately homes, and dogs—with a dash of mystery, thriller, and suspense.

My acclaimed GUIDING EMILY SERIES chronicles the life of a young woman who loses her eyesight on her honeymoon and reclaims her independence with the help of her guide dog, proving that *sometimes the perfect partner has four paws.* GUIDING EMILY was adapted for the Hallmark Channel in 2023.

If you enjoy holiday stories, be sure to check out THE CHRISTMAS CLUB (adapted for the Hallmark Channel in 2019) and PAWS & PASTRIES. They're Christmas stories of hope, friendship, and family. The story of Clara and her dog Noelle continue in SWEETS & TREATS, and SNOWFLAKES, CUPCAKES AND KITTENS.

If you're a fan of mysteries, look for the novels in my "WHO'S THERE?!" collection.

I hope you'll connect with me on social media. You can find me on Facebook, where I have a page and a special group for my readers, and follow me on Amazon, Goodreads, and BookBub so you'll know when I have a new release or a deal. You can also sign up for my newsletter at this link: https://barbarahinske.com/newsletter/

If you enjoyed this book or any of my other books, I'd be grateful if you took a few minutes to leave a short review on Amazon, BookBub, or Goodreads. Just a few lines would be great. Reviews are the best gift an author can receive. They encourage us when they're good, help us improve our next book when they're not, and help other readers make informed choices when purchasing books. Reviews keep the Amazon algorithms humming and are the most helpful aide in selling books! Thank you.

To post a review on Amazon:

1. Go to the product detail page for *Wishful Tails* on Amazon.com.
2. Click "Write a customer review" in the Customer Reviews section.
3. Write your review and click Submit.

In gratitude,
 Barbara Hinske

ABOUT THE AUTHOR

USA Today Bestselling and Amazon All Star Author BARBARA HINSKE is an attorney and novelist. She loves to read and write women's fiction, mystery/thriller/suspense, and sweet Christmas stories. She's authored the Guiding Emily series, the mystery thriller collection "Who's There?", the Paws & Pastries series, three of the novellas in The Wishing Tree series, and the beloved <u>Rosemont series</u>. Her novella *The Christmas Club* and novel *Guiding Emily* have both been adapted for Hallmark Channel.

I'd Love to Hear from You! Connect with Me Online:
Sign up for my newsletter at
BarbaraHinske.com to receive your Free Gift,
plus Inside Scoops and Bedtime Stories.
Search for **Barbara Hinske on YouTube**
for tours inside my own historic home plus tips

and tricks for busy women!
Find photos of fictional Rosemont and Westbury,
adorable dogs, and things related to my books at
Pinterest.com/BarbaraHinske.
Email me at **bhinske@gmail.com**.

Printed in Great Britain
by Amazon